I0625133

UNFAZED PUBLISHING
YOUR MIND IS OUR BUSINESS

BYRON S. DOWLING SR.

****

THE GREAT

WAR

THE CHRONICLES OF THE LION EMPIRE SERIES

TABLE OF CONTENTS

****

STORY ONE: THE GREAT WAR

WWW.UNFAZEDPUBLISHING.COM

WHAT'S YOUR STORY ?

BYRON S. DOWLING SR.

****

THE GREAT

WAR

THE CHRONICLES OF THE LION EMPIRE SERIES

UNFAZED PUBLISHING
YOUR MIND IS OUR BUSINESS

TAMPA FLORIDA

BYRON S. DOWLING SR.

ISBN: 9781959275367

Library Of Congress Number: 20244910790

Story One

- THE GREAT WAR -

"PROLOGUE"

Prophecies & Visions

****

The white lion approached the Western Temple quickly. A low thrumming panic motivating his movements. It had been a long night. An unsettling one, and he had risen before dawn to make it to the temple early in the morning as the sun rose. As he made it to the front arch of the temple, the temple master, another white lion named Y'pal, came out from the shadowed building and offered a small, almost understanding smile. "For Mother Nature," Ulan greeted, dipping his head respectfully. "For Mother Nature. Welcome back, Ulan." Temple Master Y'pal gave the younger lion a serene smile. "What brings you back to the Western Temple?" "Forgive me for not giving notice, Master Y'pal," Ulan said, looking at the master with troubled eyes, "but I have had a dream." Y'pal's smile faded, but there was no surprise in his eyes as Ulan had expected. "A troubling dream, I see." He stepped to the side. "Come in, please." Ulan followed Y'pal inside where candles lit the hallway they walked down. Glossy floors reflected the candlelight in strange patterns along the walls, and the grand marble statues of Mother Nature's highest gods acted as pillars holding up the roof. Any other day, Ulan would have marveled at the awe of this temple which he visited often. Today, though, there were much more important things on his mind. The hallway led down to an arched open doorway. Even from a distance, Ulan could see the grand statue of Mother Nature and the altar underneath her peaceful smile. At the altar, another body knelt before the statue. "You are not the only one who has had a troubling dream," Master Y'pal added. "I feel the two must be connected somehow."

Ulan followed the temple master through the archway and into the temple room. When Master Y'pal stopped, he turned and nodded to Ulan. Ulan continued up to the figure kneeling at the altar, their robe covering up their markings. The figure started to turn as Ulan approached, then rose to their full height, removing their hood, and revealing themselves as Ulan came up beside them. A tiger. "For Mother Nature," the tiger spoke, joining his paws before himself. Ulan followed suit. "For Mother Nature." "It's been a long time, Ulan," the tiger expressed. "Kiel." Ulan assessed the tiger's spiritual leader. "Master Y'pal tells me you have had a troubling dream as well?" "Yes," Kiel answered solemnly, "a very troubling dream. You must listen, Ulan. What I tell you, I believe comes from Mother Nature herself."

CHAPTER ONE

EMPEROR AS'KAI'S SONS

****

"What is your purpose?"

A light breeze passed over the land as two lion cubs looked over the edge of the cliff to the great plains of Africa. "To protect and lead Africa into the future," the cubs uttered in unison. "And how do you do that?" their father, Emperor As'kai, asked in his powerful voice behind them, his golden-tan mane billowing in the breeze. "With wisdom, power, and a just heart," the cubs replied. "Very good," their father responded smiling. "So you do listen to your dad after all." The siblings looked up at their father as he grinned down at them. Rael, the older of the twins, looked back with determination and pride, while his minutes-younger brother, Geo, looked back over all of Africa. "Will we really become emperors of all of this?" Geo asked, his high-pitched voice laced with wonder and awe.

As'kai hesitated, "One... of you will...," he says softly to his sons. The cubs' attention went to their father. "What do you mean, Father?" Rael asked. As'kai looked down at his sons once again. "Traditionally, only one male lion has been born to take the place of the emperor; heir to the throne. Any sons born after the first were just sons. Valued, of course, but not heirs. But with you cubs, the two of you were born at the same time; twins. So it will be between the two of you who is to be emperor." Rael and Geo looked at each other. "What if we both want to be emperor?" Geo asked. As'kai gracefully settled next to them and looked out over his empire. "Well, you will have to settle that between the two of you." "You mean, there have never been twins like us before?" Rael asked. Again, As'kai hesitated. "There have..." "How did they settle it back then?" Rael pressed. As'kai looked down at his cubs' questioning faces, sighed, and looked back at the terrain. "Perhaps it would be better to talk about that another time, on another walk." He motioned with a head out to the land. "Look." The cubs looked to see a pack of lionesses far in the distance, heading out into the land. A cloud passed over the sun, shading them as they walked toward the forest. "Where are they going?" Rael asked. "To hunt food for the pride," As'kai answered. "Without you, Father?" Geo asked, concern coloring his words. As'kai chuckled deeply. "Yes. The Transvaal lionesses are known for their skill as hunters. There has never been a day, and never will be one, where I could outhunt even one of them; let alone when they hunt as a unit." As'kai looked back to his sons. "You must never forget how important the lionesses are to the emperor. In exchange for protection and leadership, they provide food and support. You must always respect and honor them, and they will honor and support you." The cubs nodded, looking out at the lionesses again as they inched towards the forest. "Good luuuuuuck!" Rael yelled out towards them. As'kai laughed. "From this far away, they will never hear you son, but you can trust me when I say that they will make you a proud lion." Geo sat down beside his brother, "So what do we do now? Just wait for them?" As'kai nodded once. "They will return home when they are ready." He rose to his feet. "For right now, I must take care of all of my own duties, such as checking on the rest of the pride. Would you like to come?" The twins jumped up shouting, "Yes!" being excited. That brought another deep chuckle out of As'kai. "Alright," he said, "last one home takes a bath first tonight!" Then he took off bounding over and down the hill, away from the ledge that let them oversee the land and towards their home. His cubs yelled as they ran after him. As'kai slowed his speed to give his cubs a chance to catch up, and when they did they taunted him, telling him he was old and slow. He wondered where they had learned to talk in this manner.

It didn't take them long to reach the bottom

of the Great Hills where they butted up against the grand cliff face that led up into a beautifully ornate castle. Built directly into the rock face, the door yawned before them, leading into the main entryway of the castle. Beyond it was a winding hallway that led upwards into a variety of chambers and rooms where the generals, sentries, and pride members slept. The throne room sat at the highest point, the dining room at the lowest, with the emperor, queen, and cubs' chamber directly in the middle so they were never without defenses above or below them during an attack.

Seeing their victory, the cubs sped up ever so slightly toward the main entrance. Their twelve-year-old legs carrying them into the doorway as they shouted they had beaten the emperor, that he would have to bathe first. Those that were hanging around in the common areas of the castle—a castle that housed all members of the pride, rather than just the royals—chuckled as the young cubs passed, giving As'kai kind smiles, bowing lowly as he followed his sons through the doors. As'kai chuckled after the cubs, nodding to the pride members as he passed them. However, a tightness fell into his chest as his eyes fell on Ulan, the spiritual leader of the Transvaal Pride. He was sitting just before the winding hallway that led up into the better parts of the castle, beyond the dining and common areas, waiting for him. As the cubs ran past him, up towards their chamber to get cleaned up from their day out with their father, Ulan stood. The dark grey of Ulan's mane was in perfectly subtle contrast to his slender, silver body as he approached the emperor, trouble weighing in his eyes. Still, despite the weight that the emperor could see sitting on his shoulders, Ulan walked with grace and elegance. "Your Majesty," Ulan addressed, giving a bow to his emperor. "Ulan," As'kai stated. "For Mother Nature." "For Mother Nature, emperor." He raised his head. "To what do I owe the pleasure?" "Forgive me for coming unannounced, your highness, but I have urgent news that couldn't wait. I must speak with you immediately." As'kai didn't like the sound of that. "What's this about, Ulan?" "Your Highness, I fear that the empire is in great danger."

*****

"The sons of As'kai will lead the pride to great prosperity and wealth among the empire," Ulan began. The two lions were now high above the rest of the pride, situated in the throne room of Emperor As'kai where he had gathered the Transvaal Pride's small circle of advisors. Ku'tem, the queen of the pride, sat just to As'kai's left. Ulan continued, "Together, they will rule with great wisdom and strength, as their father guided them to." Emperor As'kai glanced at his wife. "Ulan, forgive me, but I do not see this as an issue," The Queen added. "To be seated at the throne, My Queen, there is a threat that first must befall the present emperor. An evil already works to gain strength, even now, to challenge the leadership of the emperor. A tiger." "The tigers are scattered throughout the land. They are no threat to us." Emperor As'kai declared, "A new tiger will rise up and unite them, your highness," Ulan insisted, "and gain help from others as well, though it is not so clear. They will become the greatest threat the pride has ever seen. It is in the stars. One of the other leaders and I have seen it." Emperor As'kai assessed his wife, who was clicking her claws on the armrest of her throne weighing Ulan's words. "Are the tigers active right now?" She asked the spiritual leader. "The renegade has not yet begun his conquest. I do not know who, just when and what he will do." Ulan informed the royal couple. "How are we to prepare, Ulan, with such little information?" As'kai questioned, exasperation leaking through his practiced tone of calm. Ulan bowed deeply. "I apologize, Your Majesty. I only know what

Mother Nature permits, what comes in dreams." A paw settled gently on As'kai's, and he glanced at his wife, who was looking at him softly. He took a deep breath and turned back to the white lion before them. "You're certain of this, Ulan?" Ulan met the emperor's gaze. "Yes, Your Highness." "Are we to just wait for him to show himself?" "Until then, we are to guide the cubs—your successors—to ensure they are the best emperors who they can be. I do not know the outcome of the renegade's reign. I only know that he will present...opposition. Strong opposition." Emperor As'kai nodded. "Is there anything else, Ulan?" Ulan gave the emperor a weighted look, one which communicated clearly there was more, but more that may do well to fall on fewer ears. "No, Your Highness." He said slowly. "Very well. I'd like for you to remain behind to help us discuss what is to happen with the training of the cubs. The rest of you," the emperor addressed the other members of the council, "are free to go." The council members stood and bowed gracefully to their emperor, then departed quickly. Ulan was silent until the last of their footsteps could no longer be heard down the long hallway.

"Ulan." The emperor's voice was edged in worry. "There was much emphasis on the ascension of my cubs during this discussion…and though you do not know the outcome of the attack, you do know something of it, do you not?" The spiritual leader hung his head. "Yes, sire, and it is news I wish I did not know and did not have to share." As'kai's face fell, but he nodded. Ulan continued, "The tiger that threatens our lands is young yet, unpracticed. There is some hope, though it is slim, that we might be able to persuade him to goodness if Kiel can find him in time. Kiel was able to see enough to know the young tiger is motivated by hatred, and revenge, for the murder of his parents. Rogue lions were responsible for their deaths it seems, and he now holds all of us at fault. He intends to reclaim the debt to their lives by claiming control of the throne and all of the plains. We hope Kiel will find him in time. We pray he's able to give him the proper spiritual guidance which will persuade him away from this choice and what we have seen will not come to pass." As'kai and Ku'tem shared a glance. They knew Ulan was doing his best, but that which was already prophesized would come true. Prophecies of this nature might as well have been written in stone. "What is it that you have seen, Ulan?" Ku'tem asked. "In detail." Ulan sighed. "I have seen as I have spoken. A tiger comes, bearing threat to the pride, and he comes with an army—one that is not yet clear. There will be a battle, the outcome of which I am still unsure of. But during that battle, your princes will take the throne." Ulan finally raised his head. "Whatever is to come, your highness, you are not to survive it." Ku'tem took a sharp breath. As'kai cleared his throat. "How long until then, Ulan? Until the tiger comes?" Ulan shook his head. "We are hoping to know more once Kiel actually finds the tiger, but he has not yet located him." "Very well," As'kai said softly. "So we prepare the cubs until then." "Yes, Your Highness." "We begin tomorrow." As'kai eyed Ulan carefully. "It would be my honor if you would teach them the ways of nature, Ulan. More than I would ever be able to." Ulan nodded. "Of course, Your Highness." "Thank you. We will set you up with a room both for yourself and your family." Ulan's head hung just a bit as he said, "It is only me and Imena now." As'kai nodded. "I am very sorry for your loss, my friend. You and your daughter may stay here for as long as you would like. There will always be a room for you." Ulan bowed graciously and thankfully. "I will return as soon as I receive more information." Then he was gone.

Ku'tem and As'kai remained behind, silent for a long time, until Ku'tem finally turned to her husband. "As'kai," she whispered. "There is risk in ruling, Ku'tem. We knew this from the time I was a cub. There is risk for them too. If there is nothing to be done for me, then we must do everything we can for them. So I will not dwell on it. I will train our cubs. I will prepare them. And when the time comes for this conflict, I will not go willingly or easily, I promise you." Ku'tem's paw returned to her husband's as she encouraged him, "Do not fear. You are doing well to prepare them for when their time comes to take over the pride. When this opposition comes, I have no doubt they will be ready." As'kai placed his paw over his wife's, comforting her, and trying to receive comfort from her as well. However, fear boiled in his stomach unfettered. What if they weren't prepared well enough? Would this renegade be the end of the Transvaal Pride? Ku'tem had tears in her eyes, but they did not fall as she declared, "You are a mighty emperor, As'kai." "Our sons will be even mightier."

CHAPTER TWO

CROSSING BOARDERS

****

"That's everyone."

"Good."

Na'uul, leader of the Jaal Pride, looked to his second in command, Waerik, seated to his left, and then to the other four lions in the room — his three generals and his son, seated at his right hand. They were all situated around a large oval table inside the strategy room within the castle of the Jaal Pride, the second largest pride on the plains. A map of the territories sat splayed on the table in front of them, untouched and unneeded for the conversation Na'uul wished to have with them that day. Na'uul began, "Brothers. For far too long, we have lived under the thumb of the Transvaal Pride's rule. Now, the time has come for us to rise up to reclaim our power, our right to the throne." The generals' expressions did not change as they

stared stoically at him. "Word has come," Na'uul continued, unphased by their lack of reaction, "that the tigers across the lands have birthed a leader of rebellion. The spiritual leaders have seen it, and my eyes across the plains have confirmed that an orphan roams, seeking revenge on the lions for claiming the lives of his parents." A small smirk curved the corner of Na'uul's mouth. "What does a tiger hunting lions have to do with our uprising?" One general asked. Myre. "I agree. If he's hunting lions, we should be on our guard, not celebrating," another general, Jorel, agreed. Na'uul's smirk widened into a wicked grin. "Generally, yes. But there are two things in this scenario that befit us, Jorel, that I would beg you, beg all of you, to pay attention to. We have been living in the shadow of the Transvaal Pride for centuries. Soon, we will be able to prove that they do not belong in power. And soon, the rightful emperor will be seated on the throne. Let us take a note from history. It is the strongest who should lead,

not the closest to the current emperor by blood. He who has the ability, not he who has the bloodline." "But what has this to do with the tiger and us, Na'uul?" Jorel pressed. "With the tigers on our side, we have more of a leg up on the Transvaals," Na'uul informed his generals. "With their help, we have the chance and ability to take the throne, more so than we ever have. We will have strength as well as numbers." "Will we truly have enough bodies?" Ex'ne, the final general, asked. He was the best battle strategist that Na'uul had ever seen. He thought in numbers, in war maps, and was always ten steps ahead when it came to battle. "If it were a matter of a few, it wouldn't be an issue, but the Transvaals have a vast army. A few rogue tigers and our army compared to the Transvaals will not match up." Na'uul chuckled. "The Transvaals have not engaged in combat in a century. Their army is practiced only in performance. They have numbers, but they lack skill, the same as their leader. Though they may train now with news of a new threat, we have surprise on our side. If they do not know that we are coming, then they will most likely not prepare their masses. With us and the tigers, it should be enough to overcome them." "I don't see how you can know that," Ex'ne continued. "Have you spoken with this tiger? Do you know of his numbers?" "Enough," Na'uul snarled. "The tiger cub has yet to rise. But when he does, it is predicted that all tigers on the plains will side with him. Though vast, there are many. The tigers will come to his aid, and we will also. A mutually beneficial aid to a mutually desired goal: the downfall of the Transvaals." "The tiger seeks to overthrow all lions," Myre added in. "What makes you think he will ally with you?" "He needs numbers, and he seeks to gain control by going to the top. If he overthrows the top and has allied with the second largest pride on the plains, the rest will fall in line. He will have the control he desires, and we will have the control we desire." Na'uul's patience was growing thin.

Finally, there were no other questions. Though the lions around the table looked generally displeased with this line of discussion, they seemed to be unable to come up with any other rebuttals. "Our day is coming, brothers. But the time to strike is now, when there is another threat present to distract them. Dismissed." The generals got up at the command of their leader and filed out of the strategy room. Na'uul stood by the door and watched as his men departed. Waerik was the last to leave, giving his leader a meaningful look as he went, and then nodding solemnly and shutting the door behind him as he went. When Na'uul turned back around, he was surprised to find his son, Nayme, still seated at the table, staring at the same spot that he had been focused on throughout the entirety of the meeting. "Nayme," Na'uul said as he reapproached the table. "Is there something on your mind, son?" Nayme sighed, appearing to war with himself over speaking up, but after a long moment, he finally turned to his father and said, "I don't quite understand this, Father. This... desire to overthrow them. We live in peace. There has been no war. There is no in-fighting." "There is no war or fighting because they are so large, Nayme. It is unbalanced." Nayme shook his head. "It doesn't seem right. And besides, siding with the tigers? Father, he will not honor this allyship. You will be betrayed." "Nayme, you are young, barely beyond a cub. I asked you here to learn. As my heir, it is important that you know our allies and our conflicts. This tiger solves much of the issue of tension we have with the Transvaals. As it is your first meeting with the generals, I would advise you to listen and to learn." "I'm eighteen, Father, a lion by any right. And as you heir, I should have as much, if not more, say than Waerik." "You will when you are ready. That time is not now. Now run along." Nayme eyed his father for a long time, then exhaled deeply and nodded his head. He submitted, but his eyes still held that same worried, disappointed look. "I will see you tomorrow, Father." He left the room, being sure to latch the door behind him. Na'uul watched after his son for a long time, turning over the words in his head. But then he shook it, and the words were gone. He was doing this to better the prides. The tigers were weak in numbers, and the Jaal were strong in body. They would never be overpowered by the tigers in such a way. Their only logical choice was to side with them. Alone in the room at last, Na'uul took a deep, satisfied breath. He approached the window on the far side of the room, through which blew a warm summer breeze that ruffled his dark tan mane as he peered out over the rest of his camp, taking it all in. Dilapidated houses dotted the land as far as he could see. Dirt roads connected neighborhoods to one another, if they could even be called that. Sectors were divided only by who was poorer, not who had more riches. He made promises to himself then, that when he came into power, none of his people would live in squalor. All would live in the lap of luxury they so rightly deserved.

CHAPTER THREE

WHERE TIGERS ROAM

****

The tiger's spiritual leader Kiel was on a trek back from the Western Temple, one of many he had taken in the last few weeks while meeting with Temple Master Y'pal and Ulan, when he crossed paths with a young tiger on the side of the road. The tiger appeared to have been in a fight, with torn clothing, a nasty cut that ran across the length of his jaw, and a bandage dirtied halfway hanging off of his paw. Kiel's blood was chilled as he approached. "For Mother Nature," Kiel said to him softly. "I do nothing for the Mother, for she has done nothing for me," the young tiger proclaimed. Kiel's forehead crumpled at his words. What had happened to such a young soul for him to feel so angry towards Mother Nature so soon in life? Kiel took another step forward, resting a paw on the tree the tiger lay besides. As he did so, a vision flashed through his head: the young tiger before him crying out as two lions barreled across the path, taking the lives of his parents as they went. It was the vision that had sent Kiel to the temple so many months ago, only expanded; the reason why the young tiger sought to go after the lions in the first place. The vision continued as Mother Nature showed Kiel the young tiger's fight which led him here, to this spot on the road, tending to his wounds. The fighting style he used, the stances, were wild and unpracticed, raw and unforgiving. Keil's heart hurt for him, but his head pounded. He had to get this information to Ulan and Y'pal as soon as he could. He found the tiger. "Son," Kiel said softly. "I know your pain." The tiger turned his head away, scoffing. "I don't want your pity, sir, but thank you." "It is not pity; it is compassion. Grief is vast and hard. Let me help. I am a guide for spirits and the spiritual. Let me use my gifts to get you to the other side of this hurt." The tiger shook his head. "There is no other side." Kiel nodded, sitting down against the tree a bit away from the young tiger. He was still young, Kiel observed, perhaps nearly eighteen or a little older. A little older than the princes the Transvaals held so dearly to them, who just now crested thirteen. "When I was your age," Kiel started, clearing his throat once and then repeating himself, "when I was your age, the temple folk came for me. One of the old masters of the spiritual temple in the east told me that in order to come to my full power, I needed to live and breathe Mother Nature's teachings. I was taken from my family. By the time my teachings were finished, and I was a spiritual leader, fit to take the place of Kieran, the former tiger in my place, my parents had passed away from an illness which ran rampant in my village. I never even got to say goodbye to them." The tiger was looking at Kiel now. Something like disbelief in his eyes, but it wasn't anger, and it wasn't distrust, Kiel noted. "How come you kept the faith, if they took you like that?" Kiel smiled softly. "Because through my faith, I feel them. My parents — all the dead — are in nature around us. If you listen, you can hear them in the way the wind blows or the grass sings." The young tiger raised an eyebrow. "That kind of seems..." Kiel chuckled. "No one ever believes me until they try. What do you say, young one? What's the hurt in a little practice? If it doesn't work, you've done nothing but had a warm bed and a nice meal for a time, hmm?" The tiger sized Kiel up again. "Isn't this just your job?" "You get paid to do jobs, son. This is what I love." Kiel stood and started walking in the direction of the tiger villages in the east, where his home resided on the outskirts. "I have messages to deliver to the temple, but they can wait until tomorrow. Come along. We can get you cleaned up and get something to eat." Kiel didn't turn, but he was pleased — and greatly relieved — when he heard the young tiger's paws padding after him.

*****

The tiger's name was Zelnir, Kiel learned this on their way to his hut, located on the far side of one of the tiger villages. He introduced himself quietly as they walked, after a long silence had perhaps prompted the need within him to fill it. "It's nice to meet you, officially, Zelnir. My name is Kiel." "I know," the tiger replied, "I've seen you around. My parents and I, we used to live in this village." "I see," Kiel responded, nodding slightly. Slowly, Zelnir started to reveal how he ended up by himself on the side of the road. He had been searching for the lions that hurt his parents, he informed Kiel. He wanted revenge. It had been years since it occurred, but he was bigger now, stronger. He'd Tried at first to heal, but no amount of time would make that hurt go away. He had learned a few fighting moves from some tigers he'd met in passing, stayed with them for a few weeks while he picked up the skill, then went on his way, back towards where he knew the lions lived. "This morning when you found me," Zelnir told Kiel, "I had been in a fight with some other tigers over a place to sleep. I lost." His eyes were downcast. "I spent the night half-awake against that tree, terrified I was going to get attacked by another set of lions." "Well, never mind that now. You won't have to fight for a place to sleep anymore." Zelnir nodded. After a long pause, he asked, "How are you going to help me, Kiel?" "I am going to teach you how to channel nature, to find peace, to defend yourself if you need to in your travels, and to be able to hear your parents, to know they are around you. My goal, my hope, is to help you grieve, young one." Zelnir nodded. "Thanks. I think." Kiel replied only by smiling.

When they reached Kiel's hut, both were tired from the long walk. They cleaned themselves, had supper together, and then lounged in their respective rooms. Kiel set aside some space for the young tiger when they'd arrived. He was hoping Zelnir might tie down some of that anger, that distrust, by having his own area inside the hut. For several days, Kiel gave Zelnir space when he needed it which allowed him to acclimate to life within the hut and returning to his childhood village without his parents. Kiel brought him into town on his trips, introduced Zelnir to some of the elder tigers, and watched as he reconnected with some of the tigers which were his friends before he'd left. When he felt confident Zelnir, at the very least, would not run while he was away, Kiel informed him he had to make a few day's trek to the Western Temple to communicate with the temple master there. He told Zelnir when he returned they would begin their training at once, to help him in any way he could. Zelnir nodded. "Would you mind, Kiel, if I went to the village while you were gone? It was... nice... to see some of my friends again." "I think that's a wonderful idea, Zelnir." They exchanged their goodbyes, and Kiel left that night for the temple.

Master Y'pal was waiting for him at the arches when he arrived nearly twelve hours later, as always. The master always seemed to know when the spiritual leaders were coming. They exchanged greetings, and Master Y'pal led Kiel inside to one of the chambers where they could speak privately. The spiritual tiger quickly revealed to the lion all he had encountered over the last few days: finally meeting the rogue tiger and the progress he already made over such a short period of time. He even shared the hope he held close to his heart about the situation. He asked if Ulan made it back. Kiel asked Y'pal to share the information with him once he returned. Y'pal agreed. Tired from his journey, Kiel spent the night at the temple and made the return trek in the morning, leaving the master with a reminder to get his message to Ulan. Reminding Ulan nothing would be done until they knew whether Zelnir stayed, left, or accepted Mother Nature. Y'pal nodded at every word then watched his retreating figure until

Kiel couldn't see the temple over the plateaus anymore.

When he returned to the village that evening, he found Zelnir out and about with his friends, a girl hanging closely beside him. They were laughing, enjoying themselves. Hesitant to interrupt, Kiel waited until Zelnir turned to him, then gave him a small wave to let him know he returned and retreated to the hut. It was not until some hours later when Zelnir also returned. Kiel heard him collapse into bed and did not try to sleep himself until he heard soft snores coming from the young cat's room.

*****

The next several months went by, they were in much of the same routine. In the morning, they would have breakfast. After breakfast, Kiel would lead them both in a morning prayer to Mother Nature. They would take in the sun, show appreciation for the vegetation, and give thanks for any water they might find for that day. Then Kiel would bring Zelnir through a series of defense poses, gracefully correcting his stance where it went wrong and giving him the tools he needed to turn an attacker's energy against themselves, rather than harming himself or causing injury they did not make for themselves. They would share supper, again sharing a prayer of appreciation for all of the things Mother Nature had given to them that day, and then go to sleep.

There were times in the middle of the day when Kiel would lead a mediation. Sometimes Zelnir tried, but Kiel knew the young cub was still caught in his thoughts. The spirals he sometimes fell into were written on his face. With time, Kiel believed, the peace would come. It was about a year later when Kiel started to notice things were not shifting the way he had hoped. Zelnir took to the training as he was supposed to—learning the techniques, the defenses, all of that correctly and swiftly. However, when it came to connecting with the nature around him, there was something off about the power, something wrong. While he was skilled with it, almost as natural as any spiritual leader might be, the imprint of his magic was darker, the weight of it heavier. It set Kiel ill at ease. Zelnir spent more time down at the village and less time training. He started being secretive about where he was going, and who he was with. On several occasions, he didn't come home at all. Kiel grew worried, but with no dreams from Mother Nature to warn him and no sign of any of the conflict which loomed over the plains from the year before, he had nothing he could do except wait and trust Mother Nature knew what was to happen. It was the first time, besides being taken by the temple folk, that he ever felt betrayed by her.

One night nearly a year after taking Zelnir in, the young tiger did not come home. The same panic and worry that always filled Kiel when he refused to return home filled him, but with nothing to do except trust, he went to sleep. In sleep, the dream came. It was a vivid image, one of fighting, death, decay, and destruction. When Kiel awoke the next morning, panic choked him. Zelnir's bed was still empty, the younger tiger having not returned during the night. Kiel rose quickly, foregoing his morning routines to get to the village as quickly as possible, fearing the worst. In the village, the worst met him. The tigers which lived in the village roamed about casually, as if nothing had changed. The older tigers made their way out to their daily tasks while the younger ones gathered in the village square to play. The teenagers were roaming about laughing or pushing each other around. Kiel recognized some of them as Zelnir's friends, but there was no sign of the tiger that Kiel had come to see as a son. As one of the young tigers passed by him, Kiel grabbed her arm. "Where is Zelnir, child?" he asked. She looked to him startled at first, seeming unsure of who he was or why he grabbed her. Kiel recognized her as the tiger Zelnir had been with the most, a girl he'd been hanging around with enough for Kiel to suspect she might be something more. She seemed to recognize him in the same moment, and her smile turned feline and feral. "He's gone," she said simply. "Gone?" He tightened his grip. "Gone where?" "To gather troops. To raise an army." She looked around at the two or three tigers who were around her then, and they shared her smile. "When he returns, we're to strike against the emperor. The current era of lions will fall, and tigers will rise." It was what he expected. He should have seen it coming, but he didn't. He'd been so blinded by the progress Zelnir was making, and didn't see it. The way he'd always cornered the teens, whispering to them lowly so the other tigers wouldn't hear. Even walking through the town square sneering at the older tigers. The way some of them would cower or scurry away. Kiel had been teaching him the ways of Mother Nature, and Zelnir had been using it to garner trust, or fear, to build his army. He had never been on their side. "Where is he?" Kiel demanded. Maybe if he could locate him, he could catch him before it was too late. The tigress shrugged. "He's moving across the plains. With Mother Nature on his side, there's no telling how far he's made it." One of the other tigers nodded, while the third added, "Don't bother trying to stop him. It's too late." "Too late..." Kiel echoed. He released the tigress's arm. "Go!" he nearly growled. The teenagers cackled and moved along. Kiel, though, stayed still. He closed his eyes trying to call on Mother Nature to help him with any signs of where Zelnir might be, but his mind remained blank. He sighed deeply before reopening his eyes. As he did another scan of the village, trying to plan his next moves, he saw a shift. As the teenagers turned the corner and moved out of sight, an older tiger came up to him. "Kiel, that tiger has them all convinced of this war. The entire village. You've been training him about Mother Nature, and he's been taking that power and using it to influence them to side with him. I've seen it. Good people, people who like the lions, turning against them at his word." "When did this happen?" "It's been his plan all along, Kiel," The older tiger shared softly, glancing over his shoulder as if he were being watched. "He's been poisoning their minds for months. It started with asking them if they wanted a better era for the tigers. If they truly wanted small villages or they wanted empires. Then his parents, oh their death, he used it as a negotiation tactic. Kiel, whatever he's planning, I fear they will all back him." "What of the other villages?" Kiel asked with panic creeping into his voice. "He doesn't have the time to corrupt them slowly like this." "Whatever this was, I saw his confidence grow." He nodded toward the other teenaged tigers. "With them backing him, with Mother Nature, he feels powerful and unstoppable. If they don't go with him willingly, he will take them by force. I'm sure, but he is very convincing, Kiel." Kiel looked about him at the faces of the villagers. He saw the underlying emotions in some of them, those with fear, those with hope, and those with pure and unadulterated hatred. Whatever he had done to help Zelnir, he had the awful feeling he had made it much, much worse.

CHAPTER FOUR

THE THREAT CLOSES IN

****

The year which followed the prophecy was one of great tension for the Transvaal pride, despite the emperor and empress trying to keep the information with their mounting worries from the rest of the pride members. Even as they kept the details of the prophecy contained to themselves and the few others of their council, little could be done about the whisperings. The pride being too tight knit for there to be a well-kept secret among them. They may not have known what, but all were suspect something lurked between their leaders. They were especially suspicious as Ulan and Imena moved in taking up permanent residence at the castle, rather than staying in his simple hut as most spiritual leaders do with their families; if they had families.

Each day that As'kai awakened with his sons

beside him, he thought of his impending fate, and of theirs hopelessly entwined with it. Even his sons, tried as they might play it off, started to understand something real and threatening lurked just beyond them. As'kai started training them, at first mixing their lessons in with their play and as they got older, making more intentional lessons for them to follow. Up at dawn, As'kai would bring his cubs out to the rock which overlooked their lands and show them all that was theirs to inherit when the time came. He failed to mention no one knew how soon that time would be. He would discuss the different aspects of their duties as emperor: decisions which would fall on their shoulders, protections they would need to make sure stayed in place, and discussions which had to happen between them, the leaders of the other prides, and the spiritual leaders. On days when diplomacy felt like it wasn't enough, he would train them in combat. Paw-to-paw, claw-to-claw, weapon-to-weapon. "Never let your enemy out of your sights." He told them one morning while they trained, a statement that rattled viciously inside of his head. How was he to tell them not to let an enemy evade them when he could not even find his? "Don't let them get behind you, whether it's one-on-one or army-on-army combat. If they get behind you to where you can't see, they can deliver any number of fatal blows." The cubs nodded vigorously at their father's words, Geo more so than Rael. As'kai had noticed in all their training, Geo was more attentive during combat training. He liked the action and took to the steps and the combinations more readily than Rael. Both were very skilled and graceful fighters, but there was light in Geo's eyes while he did it. Rael was regal, mechanical. He listened to his father's words during their diplomatic training and knew the pride leaders as well as any of the other diplomats. As'kai knew there was no way they could both be emperor, but he saw how it might work — a fighter and a diplomat, sitting side by side on the throne. So much of his focus went into turning his cubs into royals and warriors, that at points, he forgot they were truly just cubs — barely teenagers. When they wanted to race home, he would grow confused, distressed. He couldn't understand how they could be so frivolous when so much threatened their futures. "They're young, As'kai," Ku'tem reminded him when he would voice his concerns to his wife at night, long after their sons had gone to bed. "When it is time for them to understand, they will. They are also not aware, darling, of what comes for them." Her reminder always sobered him, but always made him worry harder, and train them a little longer the next day. There were days where it was easier, though, when he did not train them so hard.

These days usually followed with updates from Ulan, when he came from the Western Temple to tell them the young tiger — Zelnir, they'd learned — was still in the care of Kiel, was progressing well, and there was still hope he would not run. Ulan made frequent trips to the temple to see if there was any news of the cub, and often returned with updates, which helped to ease at least some, if not all, of the tensions. He had been making progress with nature work, had made friends, and was settling. Kiel, it seemed, was confident with time, the cub would readapt to life in the tiger village and find forgiveness without revenge. As'kai tried not to let himself believe too deeply in hope. There had been no prophecies of peace, only of war. But hope was a fickle thing, and so were the days which Ulan came with news, he felt, things were just a little brighter around the castle.

*****

It was just past Rael and Geo's fourteenth birthday when Ulan came to the castle late at night demanding to speak to the emperor & empress immediately. He was breathing heavily, as if he had been running, and the wild look in his eyes told As'kai everything he needed to know before Ulan had even opened his mouth. Wordlessly, the three of them made their way to the throne room at the peak of the castle, summoning only their most trusted generals along the way. And then, with a confirming nod from As'kai, Ku'tem went to wake their sons. Once the seven of them were situated in the throne room, As'kai, Ku'tem, and Ulan looking panicked, Rael and Geo confused, and the generals as stoic as they always were, Ulan began to speak. "Kiel made it to the temple just yesterday." He glanced nervously at the princes, then back at the emperor, silently asking if he was sure. The emperor nodded, and the spiritual leader continued. "Zelnir has left the village. No one knows where he is. Kiel has seen nothing but war, and I have yet to see anything. There is whispering saying he looks now for allies to send back to their village." "Do we have a timeline?" "There was speculation of a week before they returned to the village to rally."

Ku'tem leaned forward. "What is it that is really scaring you, Ulan?" Ulan swallowed deeply. "Your Highness, there is nothing concrete, but as Kiel described the dream which he had, it seemed as if... well... I fear that... the war is coming. I believe the tiger has gone to recruit the other tigers across the plains to his cause. However, it is not just tigers that he will have on his side." Now the emperor was sitting at attention. "What are you saying, Ulan?" "Your highness, I fear that—I fear that there may be lions on his side as well." As'kai's blood ran cold hearing those words, and he stood abruptly. "Ulan, when is he supposed to attack? When are these lions supposed to go to him?" "I don't know, sire, you know these dreams can be very nonspecific at times." As'kai turned to his generals. "I want you to send men to hunt him down. Kill him. I don't want him to gain any more footing than he already has." "Sire," Ulan said at the same time that Ku'tem called, "As'kai." As'kai shook his head. "This tiger means to rip all lions apart at the seams, and I won't have it." He turned to his sons, anger plain in his eyes. "This is what it means to be emperor, sons, to do what is best for the greater good." He turned back to the generals. "Find him! Now! Do not return until you have his head."

*****

It was three more days before they heard any word of the lions As'kai sent after the tiger. As'kai also sent messengers to all of the other prides, requesting council with the leaders to discuss the betrayal Ulan had mentioned. Replies to the request came swiftly from all, but the Pynme Pride, in the desert, who declined to come on account of not wanting to be involved. As'kai immediately grew suspicious of them and sent spies to watch their pride closely. The rest of the pride leaders — Velan of the Rynvye Pride by the water, Anpher of the Fenwyre Pride by the forest, and Na'uul of the Jaal Pride on the other side of the plains — were to arrive in two days-time, all with guards of their own. While they waited for the leaders' arrival, As'kai spent much of his time in the throne room, discussing all information he had kept from his sons. Rael was receptive, understanding the secrets which needed to be kept in order to keep them and the pride safe, but Geo didn't want to hear it. He stalked off often, brooding, hiding. He was often found hours later in the training room, sweat slicked on his fur. He refused to speak to anyone, save for his brother and sometimes Imena, whom the princes had grown up and grown close with.

It was two days of tension in the rest of the pride as well, as they were informed of the other pride leaders' arrival and a feast was prepared for their coming. It was not often so many powerful people were in one place, and despite the reason and the tension, many of the younger lions were curious and excited to see what would come of it all. The night before the leaders were to arrive, one of the generals returned, bloody and soaked from the rain outside. The emperor had seen him approaching, seen as the people in the castle commons ran to the general's aid, and watched as someone came running to collect him and Ulan. As'kai followed the lion down the hallway to the main foyer where the general lay, battered and still actively bleeding. "Your highness," The general said, his voice ragged, his breathing shallow. "Emperor As'kai, you must prepare. The tiger, he is much stronger than we anticipated. And he is not alone. The tigers that back him, they are... they are set on this. They mean to kill us all." "General, where are the rest of your men?" "He killed them, your highness, he killed them all. He only let me live so that I could deliver a message. He says he is coming. And when he comes, the lions must submit or die." As'kai took in the general's face for a long time, and then nodded solemnly. "Ulan, get him to the infirmary." The spiritual leader complied. As'kai remained behind, staring out of the main entrance of the castle into the rain, one of the few rain showers the plains ever saw. Ku'tem came beside him, placing a paw on his shoulder. "As'kai..." "The pride leaders get here tomorrow. We will have our meetings, try to discover who the dissenters are. Then once they've departed, I'm going after the tiger myself." "As'kai..." "...It's not up for debate, Ku'tem. I will do whatever I can to keep our sons safe." "What if saving them is going to put your life in danger? What then?" the empress questioned. "It is no longer about me," As'kai expressed. "Ulan has already seen that whatever this conflict is, I will not make it out alive. I do not know when I shall die, but if I am to, then I will do as I said before — not go easily nor willingly. And I will put our sons first." "Please," Ku'tem begged. "It is not up for debate. I will prepare to leave after the leaders have all left. Now off to bed. Tomorrow is a long day." The queen nodded, and together the royal couple retreated to their chambers. Though their breathing remained even and their room remained quiet, neither of them slept the entire night.

CHAPTER FIVE

THE ARRIVAL OF THE PRIDES

****

The Transvaal Pride members set the castle up like they were preparing for The Festival of the Plains and not a diplomatic event. That first day, there was hustle and bustle everywhere as people cooked and cleaned and decorated for the arrival of the leaders from the other prides. Some of the lions had never seen leaders of the other prides before. It was so rare that the leaders met in person at times there were entire generations of lions who had never even met those from other prides. This meeting, despite being one of a grave reason, was a momentous event.

The first of the leaders, Anpher, arrived just after midday. His pride, Fenwyre by the forests, was closest to the Transvaals, just beyond them to the west. He came with his wife and their two most trusted guards. Even as allies for many years, with so much talk of unrest, one could never be too careful, and As'kai didn't fault him for that. When Anpher arrived, As'kai offered him a wide smile. "Old friend," he addressed to the other lion leader, stepping forward with an extended paw. "As'kai," Anpher said, stepping in to take the emperor's paw, and then pulling him in for a hug and clapping him on the back. "It has been many years." "Too many." Anpher nodded, then stepped back and pulled his wife forward. "As'kai, please meet my wife, Mikani." "A pleasure to meet you," As'kai expressed, shaking her paw. He introduced Ku'tem in the same fashion. Greetings were then exchanged between the Fenwyre leader and Ulan, and then As'kai introduced his sons. "Ah, the heirs. I have been hearing much about you two cubs lately," Anpher shared, shaking Rael and Geo's paws. "Tell me, children, have you decided who is to rule?" Rael and Geo shared a glance and then looked back at Anpher. "We are to rule together, sir," Rael informed him. Anpher let out a deep-seated laugh. "There are legends of twins. I've always wondered if we would get to see it play out in this lifetime." "Anpher!" As'kai warned. The Fenwyre leader held up his paws in submission. "Apologies, Your Highness." He turned back to the princes. "My apologies to you too cubs, if I have offended you in any way." Rael and Geo nodded in acknowledgement of his apology, but notably did not forgive him. It would be remembered. By the emperor, too, from the look on his face. The three lions shared a look. They would be watching Anpher, though Unmir, the leader of Pynme by the desert who declined their invite, was still at the top of the list. Seated farthest away from the castle and pride, they were the least connected to the rest of the lions, the most likely to defect, and the most likely to have committed the murders that started all of this in the first place. As'kai's spies had yet to report anything, however, so they were still watching the other pride leaders closely. "I will have someone show you to your rooms. There will be a feast tonight in honor of all of your arrivals, once all of the leaders arrive. If you are hungry now, I can have someone send something up for you if you'd like as well," As'kai stated. "No, we're fine, thank you. Getting settled and perhaps a little rest will do us good before what I'm sure is to be a political bloodbath come the morning." As'kai's face fell only slightly. "Yes, I'm sure tomorrow is to be something for the generations." He waved off into the crowd towards one of the guards waiting there. "Can you please bring Pride Leader Anpher and his wife Mikani to their room?" "Yes, Emperor As'kai." The guard bowed to the new leader in his presence and then headed towards the back of the main room, where the hallway would lead them higher into the castle. The royal families said their goodbyes. Anpher and his wife followed the guard to their quarters. As'kai turned to his wife and sons, eyeing the princes cautiously. "Anpher is an old friend, but he always wants attention. I don't believe he wishes for my death, but he..." "...We heard what he said," Rael cut in, "about wanting to see the twins seated." "As'kai, you can't really think..." Ku'tem started, but As'kai cut her off. "...I don't know what I think, Ku'tem. All I know is the only people I truly trust, at this moment, are standing here speaking with me. So I would caution you these next few days." "Yes Father," Geo answered. Rael echoed him. "I don't know when the next leader is to arrive, but I would expect you both to be here." "Yes Father," the princes repeated.

The princes departed from there, to where As'kai could only assume, but he and Ku'tem remained in the main foyer of the castle, awaiting the arrival of the other leaders. Tension rolled off of As'kai's shoulders in waves so thick he was surprised his wife did not drown in them. "This will all work out, As'kai," she said softly after a long while. "Ulan has predicted I am to die, Ku'tem." Her breathing hitched a little, but she remained as steady as he had ever seen her. "We will do everything in our power to prevent it from happening. If we cannot…" "…We will do everything we can to protect our sons." "Exactly." "You never asked for this, and for that I am sorry." "I knew what I was getting into when I married a prince, As'kai. When I bore princes." "It has not been like this for a century, Ku'tem. We had no way of knowing." As'kai stated, facing her with pain in his eyes. She placed a paw on his downturned shoulder. "You said it yourself. There is always risk." "Still, I am sorry." She placed a kiss on her emperor's cheek, soft and sweet. "None of this is your fault. But if you must hear it, you were forgiven a long time ago, my love." He nuzzled her. They stayed nuzzled for a long time with the emperor soaking in the warmth and strength of his empress, and the empress giving all that she could to an emperor who was destined to die.

*****

The other two leaders arrived just before dusk within several minutes of each other. Na'uul, leader of the Jaal Pride just across the plains, came in first, a smile as broad as the savannah itself set on his face. He came flanked by his son, Nayme, on his right, and his daughter Nara who was about the same age as the princes, on his left. Behind them stood two generals: Waerik, Na'uul's second in command, and Ex'ne, the leader's best battle strategist. They stood stoic as guards at the back of the pack, watching their royal family the same as the guards behind the Transvaal royals watched theirs. "Na'uul," As'kai uttered coolly. "Thank you for coming." They exchanged greetings and introductions across the families. "Where is your wife?" Ku'tem asked, scanning his crowd. Na'uul hung his head slightly. "She passed shortly after Nara was born, during a hunting accident." "Oh, I am so sorry to hear this," Ku'tem replied, offering a paw on his shoulder for comfort. Na'uul nodded his thanks and turned back to the emperor. "So, to what do we owe the pleasure of this invitation?" "All will be explained over a feast tonight," As'kai responded, "just as soon as the last of the leaders arrive." "I believe they have all arrived." Ulan declared nodding his head towards the door. All of the royals turned their heads, watching as the last of the leaders set to attend stepped inside the door, flanked by two guards and no one else. "Velan," As'kai called. Velan did not smile as he approached the group and nodded to all of the male lions. "As'kai..., there are... a lot of us here." "I've asked all of the leaders to attend." Velan nodded and turned to Ku'tem. He held out his hand to her, kissing her fingers softly. "Empress. You're as beautiful as ever." His attention went to the princes. "And my goodness, you cubs have gotten big since the last time I saw you." "Your wife did not want to come?" As'kai asked as Velan shook hands with Na'uul and hugged the other females. "Someone had to remain behind to lead the Rynvye," Velan stated. "Not all of us are willing to leave our prides to fend for themselves." No one missed the glance thrown at Na'uul. Na'uul's returning smile was utterly feline. As'kai stepped in before the two cats started brawling right in the middle of the foyer. There were tensions between all of the leaders, but Velan and Na'uul had history which didn't need to be dealt with here or now. "Please leaders, let's save this for another day. There are more pressing matters, and it would behoove all of you to pay attention to that for the time being." Na'uul and Velan shared unkind glances and then nodded to their emperor. As'kai sent Rael to retrieve Anpher and his wife, and then lead the other two and their guarding parties to the main dining room so we can begin the feast.

The entire pride was invited to the party, and the main dining room had been setup to accommodate as much. The front of the dining room where the emperor, the empress, and their sons usually sat, had been rearranged so that a long table was now set for all of the leaders and their guarding parties. The rest of the room had perpendicular tables set for the rest of the pride members. In the middle of each table was a platter of all sorts of food freshly hunted by the lionesses specifically for this occasion. All three pride leaders smiled hungrily at the spread as they lead their respective people forward to the horizontal table and sat themselves, each of the four main leaders centered while the rest of their parties sat extended from them towards the ends of the tables. As'kai and Velan sat facing the dining room, with Na'uul across from As'kai and Anpher, who were across from Velan. As'kai stood once all of the pride members had found seats and everyone was settled. "Thank you all for coming today. Thank you to the pride leaders for making the journey to be here and hear what I have to say. I know much is going on that has not been explained, and I hope sometime soon it will be. But until then, I encourage you to eat your fill, and enjoy yourselves. There has been tension before and there will be tension again. This does not mean we cannot still enjoy good food and good company in the meantime." There was a chorus of cheers as the emperor sat back down, and then everyone dug into their meals.

The conversation remained relatively casual as they ate, but As'kai could still feel the tension and curiosity rolling off the leaders as they sat at the table. Velan, the most reserved of the leaders, remained relatively quiet during the meal. Na'uul spoke openly with Anpher, and the two laughed and joked. As'kai did his best to engage as well, but he watched them all closely and carefully. It would be here, he felt, where they would slip up and reveal something they were not supposed to. However, all through the meal, nothing out of the ordinary was revealed, and nothing even remotely suspicious came about. Down toward either end of the table, As'kai tried to see the guards conspire, look around suspiciously, anything, but they only observed in the way that guards were supposed to. Even Na'uul's children were smiling calmly and casually, talking with his sons as if they had been friends for ages. That in and of itself, As'kai felt, was suspicious for its own reasons, but unrelated to this.

At the end of the meal, empty handed but full in belly, As'kai stood and addressed the pride again. Thanking all of the general pride members for their participation and dismissing them at their leisure. When he sat back down this time, the leaders were looking at him more expectantly. "As'kai," Velan asked, speaking for what felt like the first time the entire meal, "are you ever going to tell us why we are here?" "I told you in the letters I sent, why you are here," As'kai replied. "Yes, the tiger. But why are we here? You have informed us of the threat. What is there left to say?" As'kai sighed. "I was hoping to have one night of festivities before we became diplomates once more, Velan." "We all have prides to get back to, As'kai," Anpher said. "As much as I enjoy catching up with old friends, it may be beneficial for us to get on with this as soon as possible." As'kai looked around the table and nodded. "I understand. Please, return to your chambers and rest for a few minutes. Clean yourselves or do what you must while I oversee the throne room is properly set up, and then I will have guards retrieve you so we may begin." "Thank you As'kai," Anpher replied. "You always were the most understanding of us." The leaders stood and departed, their guarding parties following. "Oh, and leaders," As'kai called after them. They turned towards him. "It would do well if what I have to say fall on as few ears as possible." The leaders glanced at their respective parties and nodded, then continued their departure. When they were through the doors and being led by guards to their rooms, Rael and Geo approached their father. "Are we to be part of this, Father?" Geo asked. "If we are to be part of whatever is coming, it would do us well to know what it is so we can plan accordingly." As'kai turned to Ku'tem, asking her a silent question, and she nodded slowly. With a sigh, the emperor turned back to his son. "Yes, Geo. I think it would be best if you were both there to hear this." Geo and Rael nodded, then followed after the leaders. "Ku'tem, I was intending to tell the leaders everything, to reveal all that we know, to see who flinches and who does not. If the twins come, they will know that I am to die." "They are going to know one way or another," Ku'tem shared. "Let them prepare." As'kai watched after his sons for a long time. "No one can prepare them for that, I fear."

CHAPTER SIX

SECRETS REVEALED

****

"Father," Nayme said as soon as Na'uul and his guarding party were inside their chambers. "Not now, Nayme," Na'uul replied to his son as he approached the back of the room to change into his more formal attire. "Yes, now. What are we doing here, Father? They have called this meeting looking for traitors, don't think they didn't. They are going to discuss the tiger in that room, and we are going to be outed. It would be in our best interest to tell them everything that we know. Spin it as us having watched him as we had heard rumblings from our own spies," Nayme detailed. "Nayme, you are young. We haven't done anything. We haven't even found the tiger yet, spoken to him. There is nothing we are hiding." Nayme's whisper was hot and angry. "What are you talking about? You're inside the castle of the man who you plan to overthrow, discussing his enemy and your ally as if he will not figure it out! You both hunt for him. You do not think your spies have crossed paths? You don't think he already knows something?" "Have you noticed that only four of the five of us are here, Nayme? Where is Unmir? From Pynme? What of that? Why is Velan so quiet?" Na'uul turned away from his son. "You are inexperienced in the way of politics, Nayme, and it would be in your best interest to sit back, shut up, and learn if you are to succeed me." "I won't," Nayme uttered, stepping back. Na'uul spun on his son. "What was that?" "I won't. If you continue to work with the tiger, if you work to overthrow As'kai and the princes, I won't succeed you." The two lions stared at each other for a long time before Na'uul broke into a calm smile. "As you like. I have your sister. I will marry her off to one of my generals and write it in stone that they will succeed me. You will be reduced to nothing with the wave of my paw with a pen. Is that what you'd like?" "They will never honor a female ascending over the male," Nayme spat. "And she is a child, Father, barely fourteen. You threaten to marry her to someone twice her age or older." He twisted his face in disgust. "I'd distrust any of the lions that would agree to something such as this." "Then do not make me do such things to her. Your dishonor will put it on her, and I would tell her as much." Na'uul's eyes flashed. "You wouldn't." "Not if you keep your mouth shut and fall in line."

There was a knock at the door. "Leader Na'uul," a guard said from the outside, "the emperor is ready for you in the throne room." "Submit, Nayme. Now," Na'uul hissed. Nayme held his father's gaze for a long moment, and then he sighed and dropped his head, dropping to a knee. "You are making a mistake, Father. I just beg that you think it through is all." "I have been thinking it through, Nayme, with my finest generals. I promise I am only doing what is best for the most." Nayme nodded, then rose to his feet. Together, the two of them headed out into the hallway to meet the guard. "My son will be joining us in the meeting, if that is okay with the emperor," Na'uul told the guard. "If he is to succeed me, he should know the happenings of the empire, should he not?" "Yes, sire," the guard answered, eyeing the two of them, then giving a short bow and turning back towards the rising hallway. The two Jaal leaders followed in silence.

*****

The other leaders were already in the room when Na'uul and Nayme entered. The throne room was situated with the emperor and empress' thrones at the head of the room, farthest from the door, and other chairs brought in for the leaders and their guests situated like an oval spread out from them. Anpher had come alone. Velan as well. As'kai had brought his sons, and Na'uul had Nayme. Ulan stood behind the emperor's chair, a permanent fixture to him since the leader's had arrived it seemed. Limited ears indeed, Na'uul thought. "Thank you for having this meeting earlier than intended," Velan expressed once Na'uul and Nayme had taken their seats. "It's my pleasure," As'kai responded, eyeing all of them. Na'uul was almost thankful that he and Nayme were the farthest from the throne. His son was so restless he was afraid this alone would give them away. He rested a calm, settling paw on his son's arm. A warning. Nayme took it and settled. "Ulan has brought to my attention as much as he could over the last year about a threat to the empire," As'kai began, scanning each of the leader's faces as he did so. Each of them were stoic, unmoved, and Na'uul did his best to keep his the same. As'kai continued. "There is a tiger who wishes to overthrow me, and unseat all lions, because of rogues on the plains who murdered his parents. And it has also been brought to my attention that at some point, he may succeed. He is going to attack here first, because his goal is to rule.

But I fear he will work his way through all of the prides. I have called you here because I need to ask you to fight with us, so he cannot take control." The leaders now shared some glances, with each other, with As'kai, and with the princes. "As'kai, you mean to tell me that this tiger is going to grow powerful enough to overthrow you? To kill you?" Anpher pronounced, worry present in his voice. As'kai was pointedly not looking at his sons as he nodded. By the way the princes started to rise from their chairs, it was clear they had not known this. "Father?" one of them said. Na'uul couldn't tell them apart. "Not now," As'kai whispered to him softly. "Just listen." Na'uul almost smiled. Perhaps he and As'kai were not so different after all. "The tigers are so small in number, As'kai. How will they even get through your armies to get to you and kill you?" Velan asked. As'kai scanned the room again. "The latest update has informed me that there will be lions on the tigers' side, traitors to the throne.

Lions who want to take the power for themselves." "Who would want to do that?" Na'uul questioned. Beneath his paw, he felt Nayme tense. "Align themselves with tigers?" "That is what I have been trying to figure out. My number one suspect at the moment is Unmir, for he refused to come." "Unmir has not come to any summons for his entire rule. The Pynme were ravished in the last war. His entire line has spent the last century rebuilding. I can't see how they would side with the tigers, or even participate in a war in general. Because it will be, won't it? A war?" Anpher asked. Na'uul could have thrown something at him, for taking the suspicions off of the missing leader like that. "For him to decline the summons of the emperor —" Na'uul started but was cut off by Velan. "— is status quo," Velan stated. "He wants no part of the empire. That means he would also want no part of its politics. The Pynme are small and secluded. They keep to themselves and have for many years." "They produce the most rogues,"

Na'uul declared. "You produce the most rogues," Velan shot back. "The Pynme take in the most rogues, give them a place to stay, feed them. They're a pride of those with nowhere else to go." Velan shot him a look that sent a chill down his spine, a look which said he knew something. Then he turned back to the emperor. "I do not suspect the Pynme." As'kai nodded. "I appreciate your council, Velan. But without them, that leaves one of you." "Forgive me for saying this, old friend, but what of you? What's to say that you would not turn the throne over to the tiger to spare your life?" Anpher announced. "My father would never cede his throne," one of the twins growled. The dark-maned one. "Geo," As'kai warned. The young lion did not remove his glare from Anpher's face. "Ask Ulan," As'kai said. "Those that serve Mother Nature see the future and cannot lie about it. I will not cede the throne. I will be killed. We just don't know how or when yet." Anpher nodded. "I merely had to pose the thought, As'kai, you know that." As'kai nodded. "You would not be one of the leaders if you were not thorough. But that is why I now have to turn it back on you. One of the people in this room is to betray the empire. At least, that is the assumption I have." Velan and Anpher nodded. "And how are we to figure out among the four of us who is to betray the empire?" Na'uul asked. "Are we to brawl right here on the throne room floor until only the emperor or the traitor still stands? Until one of us is in chains?" "No," As'kai said calmly. "I fear there is no way to know who it is. So I will simply share what I know, share my plan, and then I will hope that I see you all on my side on the battlefield." This time all three leaders nodded. "So what do you plan to do?" Velan asked. "I am going to go after the tiger myself and try to subdue him. If that fails, which I am assuming it will since Ulan still foresees a battle, I am asking that you bring your armies to fight on the side of the lions, and that you do not turn to fight with the tigers."

"Your plan is to beg us for aid?" Na'uul asked. "No, my plan is to fight regardless. I am asking you for aid and informing you because this is going to affect us all whether you want it to or not." "And you intend to die during all of this, As'kai? What is to say that we will not all die? What is to say that this will not be a bloody battle which will end in death regardless?" Velan asked. "I'm sorry, but I cannot rightfully bring my people into this knowing death is going to follow, knowing we may not even win." "I concur," Anpher stated. "What is to say that this will not kill us all?" As'kai looked defeated already, and it took everything within Na'uul not to smile. "There is nothing which will guarantee us we will win if we go up against the tigers," As'kai allowed. "We have numbers, but I do not know what else he has on his side." "I cannot go into a battle blind, As'kai. The Fenwyre have to sit this out as well, at least until more is known. We may hear of the battle and come, but..." Anpher hesitated. "There is a threat to your empire, and you choose to sit and do nothing?" Geo asked, standing behind his father. "Geo," his brother warned standing next to him. "No, I won't just sit here." The black-maned lion moved to the center of the room. "You hear of a tiger coming to kill your emperor, to take over your lands, to rule over lions, and you choose, you choose, to do nothing?" "Son, it is far more complicated..." Anpher started. "I am not your son," Geo growled. "I am his son, and heir to this throne. And if you do not fight with us, I will assume you all to be traitors when we win this battle." "Geo," As'kai warned. "You can't just let them sit out, Father," the twin declared, exasperated. "It is their choice to fight or not to fight." "And it is my choice to ally with them at the end of this. And if they are willing to let you die..." Geo's words cut off and he looked away from his father. He turned back to the leaders of the room, scanning their faces. "If they let you die," He started again, "then they are no allies of mine." The prince stalked from the room. His twin brother scanned the room, shooting a desperate look at his father, then stalked after his brother. Na'uul felt another smile tugging at his lips. Children, he thought to himself. "As'kai," Velan kindly says. "Velan, we have no idea what his numbers look like. The Transvaals have a vast army, but there is no guarantee that we can win. There is never a guarantee. However, the more we have on our side, the better our odds. And just because I die, does not mean the empire falls. You've just witnessed my heirs, the power they hold. They are strong. They have trained beneath me and Ulan since we've heard of this threat." The emperor was pleading, a sight Na'uul never thought he would see. Velan looked to Anpher, and then to Na'uul. Then slowly, he shook his head. "The Rynvye are a small pride, As'kai. If the tiger intends to fight you and then move throughout the lands, it would do us better to prepare for our own battle against them. We will not fight with you." As'kai nodded. Velan stood, bowed, and then exited the room. As'kai refused to look at him as he went. When he was gone, As'kai raised his gaze to meet Anpher's, who was holding his chin, staring at the emperor and taking him in slowly. "Please, Anpher. If he gets lions, I don't know what is to happen to the pride." Anpher nodded slowly. "I know, As'kai." He sighed deeply. "I will send warriors to aid you. Half my army. The rest must remain behind to barricade Fenwyre. If the empire falls, we must be ready for the aftermath. But I should hope it will not fall. I will send one of my guards tonight to call for them. They will be here hopefully in three days' time. I hope they arrive before that tiger does." "I will owe you my life, Anpher, thank you." Anpher's returning smile was sad. "You will have no life to pay me in, old friend." As'kai only bowed his head. After a moment of silence, the emperor turned his attention to Na'uul. "What of you, Na'uul? Will you aid us?" Na'uul looked to his son, then to Anpher, then back to the emperor, as if contemplating. "I will spare half of my armies as well. The same as Anpher. I wish to prepare. But the sooner we quell him the better. And if there are lions rallying, more numbers on the front lines is always better." As'kai smiled at him. "Thank you, Na'uul, truly. You both are aiding the empire more than you realize, I'm sure of it." "I hope so, As'kai," Anpher replied, "for if this does not help, I fear it will hurt us all." "It will be the end of us all," Na'uul agreed. As'kai nodded solemnly. "When your armies get here..." "...Treat them as your own," Anpher instructed, and Na'uul nodded in agreement. "They will be your numbers, As'kai," Na'uul added. "Thank you both. I only hope this will be enough. For the empire's sake. It has to be." The three leaders nodded. "Now if there is nothing else, I feel I need to go speak with my sons about the developments, and I apologize for their exit. This has been... difficult for them." As'kai voiced by way of dismissal. Everyone stood. "Ruling is difficult, As'kai," Na'uul said.

"Are you sure they are ready for this?" "They will have to be," As'kai said softly, and then lead them all out of the throne room.

CHAPTER SEVEN

THE END OF AN ERA

****

The leaders left the next day, earlier than intended, the same as everything else during this meeting had gone. As'kai saw them off, thanking Na'uul and Anpher again for the lions who were set to arrive in a few days' time. To Velan, he merely shook paws and then wished him safe passage home, but that was all. Geo and Rael refused to address him at all, refusing to give him any sense of comfort from Geo's threat at the throne room. The royal family watched the leaders until they were well on their way and nearly out of sight, and then As'kai revealed the final piece of the puzzle to his sons. "I am to leave tonight, to find the tiger and see if I can do away with him." He said to his twins. "Father, let me go with you," Geo pleaded. "I can fight as well as any of the guards in the army." "And yet those guards continue to fall under this tiger's claws, son," As'kai gently answered. "And what makes you think you will not?" Rael asked. As'kai did not reply. "As'kai, you mean to tell me, you are going to hunt this tiger down even though you believe you are going to die at his paw!?" Ku'tem asked feverishly. The emperor said nothing in response to the question. He merely told his family, "I leave after sunset," and headed for the hallway. "Mother, is there nothing we can do to stop him?" Rael inquired. There were tears in the empress' eyes, but she refused to let them fall. "You know how your father is. If this is what he has decided needs to happen, this is what is going to happen, and there is nothing that can be done about it." The twins looked at their mother with anger in their eyes as they watched their father's retreating form with defeat. "What are we supposed to do?" "You take up his mantel in his stead," Ulan advised, approaching them from the doorway with Imena at his side. He too, watched As'kai's retreating form. "How do we do this?" Rael requested. "The generals need to be notified of the additional numbers, and the empire needs to be notified of what is to come," Ku'tem explained soothingly. "Geo, why don't you go talk to the generals about the lions coming from Fenwyre and Jaal, and I can help you Rael with writing letters to the Pride leaders?" The boys looked at Ku'tem, then Ulan, and back before nodding. "You are going to be great emperors." Ku'tem affirmed to them around a tightness in her chest. "I wish not for this title," Geo growled. "If Father wishes to sacrifice himself over something so foolish…" "…Geo!" Rael interrupted his twin, but Geo persisted, "No brother! I won't take on a title washed in blood. There is no need for this! For any of this! I will talk with the generals, and I will do nothing more. The title — the empire — the throne — it's yours." Geo bowed to his brother, kissed his mother, and retreated towards the head general's quarters to relay the message of the coming numbers. "He can't be serious!" Rael calmly exclaimed to his mother. "He is grieving." Kutem replied, "Give him time." "Father has not died yet. There is no place for grief." "We all know what is to come. Sometimes," Ku'tem took a deep breath, stepping forward and brushing a paw over the back of her son's head, "Sometimes, that is so much harder." Rael bowed his head to his mother's touch. "He is not dead until he has died." Then he stepped out of his mother's reach and headed towards the throne room to pen his letters.

*****

As'kai left at nightfall as promised, after long and sorrowful goodbyes to his family. Ku'tem held him for a long time, tears matting her fur as she begged him softly to reconsider. His sons hugged him tightly, and each made their own promise to do everything they could to rule with honor just as he had. When it was nearly too much to bear, when he was almost convinced by them he could not go, he could stay there with them, he turned away from his family and left. Ulan stood alongside the family, holding Ku'tem as she wept. The brothers held each other as they watched their father. They watched for a long time, until he was so far they could no longer see him. As'kai turned back several times, until the door of the castle fell out of sight, and his family was nothing but a shadow to him. He knew then he would never see them again.

It was the last time he turned around. From there, he followed the injured guard's directions to where the tiger had last been seen. He traveled for a long time, what felt like hours, before he even saw a flicker of life. It started as a fire in the distance, just a twinkle of light. But as he grew closer, As'kai was able to make out bodies around it, throwing shadows as they moved around. The sound of voices and laughter came drifting down to him as well, boiling his blood and fueling him on. When he was only a few hundred yards away, he ducked into the brush, hiding himself away to scope out the tiger and the others around the open flame. There were eleven or twelve bodies who As'kai could see. He couldn't tell right away who the leader was, but it became clear after a moment's observation, when one spoke, and the others quieted down to hear him. When he gave out instructions, the others followed them without question. It took everything in him to swallow his snarl. He crept as close as he could in the cover, then checked his swords on his back, resecured the bandolier, and decided it was time to make his presence known. With a final, calming breath to himself, he stood up. He took calm and measured steps toward the group, watching as one notified the tiger next to them, until the knowledge he was there circulated around the entire group. Finally, the leader stood, shooting a wicked smile towards As'kai. Ulan's voice came to him then, with the tiger's name rattling through his memory: Zelnir. "You got my message," Zelnir proclaimed. His smile not faltering as he stepped slightly away from the group of tigers, approaching the emperor. As'kai slowed, the two cats now face to face beside the group. "You have no business murdering my lions, cub." As'kai declared lowly. "I am no longer a cub, Emperor. I would be careful how you speak to me." There was an energy that surrounded Zelnir, something familiar yet... wrong about it. The smile which accompanied his responses was utterly feline. "Tell me, were the lions that murdered my mother and slaughtered my father in cold blood yours?" "They were rogues. They live unruled on the plains." Zelnir laughed, looking over his shoulder at his companions. "An emperor who cannot control all of his subjects. Who put you on the throne?" "There have always been rogues, child. You would know this if you stayed at the village, and listened to what the spiritual leaders tried to teach you." "That old tiger didn't know anything about anything. The Mother knows only what she gives and takes. She offers nothing for us." His smile had completely faded. "Tell me, Emperor...do you like being a leader? Do you enjoy the power?" "I don't rule for the power. I rule for my people." "Please." Zelnir spat on the ground, "No one rules for the good of the people. If not for selfish reasons, why sit on the throne?" "Are you not after the throne to make it better for all tigers?" As'kai demanded. The smile he got in response was bitter, cold. "I long for the throne for what was done to my parents. But once I have it, I have it for me. With that power, everything I do with it is for me." "Then you are not fit to rule. You are no leader." Zelnir held up his hands wide, encompassing the tigers' faces who sat snarling behind him, illuminated by fire. "I'm already doing it." "I am here to end it." "So be it," He snarled.

In an instant, the young tiger was ripping across the plains toward As'kai, paws and dust flying as he ran at the emperor with his teeth bared. The tiger extended his claws as he leapt with all fours toward the emperor. As'kai met him at full force, catching the upward momentum of the tiger's approach and changing it so the tiger kept moving forward while he himself got around the tiger's back. He sent him flying further forward with a mighty kick. From behind him, As'kai heard a round of snarls as the tigers by the fire rose and approached. "NO!" Zelnir snarled at them, the fire bouncing off of his pupils horridly as he eyed each of his companions. "He's mine to deal with." "You don't have to do this, son," As'kai proclaimed loudly so all of the tigers heard him. "I am no one's son," the tiger roared, charging again. As'kai couldn't help but notice his movements were still somewhat unrefined. But what he lacked in skill, he made up for in brute strength and agility. As'kai was not an old lion, but pitted against a far younger cat than him, with only his superior skill setting him apart, they were nearly evenly matched. One wrong move and either of them could have the upper hand. As'kai redirected this charge as well, and the tiger was supposed to sprawl, but he quickly summersaulted, got to his feet, and charged again. His previous two passes had taught him something, though, and as As'kai went to redirect him a third time, the tiger dropped low and swiped for As'kai's legs, leaving a wound across the thickest part of his right thigh. The emperor roared out in pain, but kept his focus on his opponent, bringing a strong elbow down on the back of the younger cat sending him face first into the dirt. The tigers who had cheered for Zelnir's landed blow now growled. The emperor pounced on him, pinning him down, and pulled a knife from the bandolier across his chest, pressing it to the tiger's throat. "I'll give you one chance. Walk away from this. Find peace with the temples and the spiritual leaders within them. Leave death and destruction behind." "Death can only be repaid with death," Zelnir spat. "Equal payment is all that Mother

Nature allows. Isn't that what Mother Nature teaches us? Balance?" With that, the tiger stuck his free claw into the open wound on the emperor's thigh, shredding the muscles and the arteries from within. The emperor roared and released his hold just enough from the tiger beneath him, that the younger cat was able to slip free of the hold. He quickly kicked the knife from the older cat's paw, pairing the swipe with another blow aimed at the emperor's face, which he blocked. The emperor was now badly injured, the wound on his leg staining the tanned fur a brilliant red. The tigers at the fire were shouting encouragements to Zelnir as the emperor rose back to his feet. He favored his left leg, unable to put any weight on the injury, using his disbalance to throw himself toward the younger cat rather than away from him and land a swipe with his claws across Zelnir's stomach. The tiger roared out and countered with a forceful punch to As'kai's sternum. The punch landed too perfectly, with strength behind it that was not just cat-like, but more somehow. As'kai huffed out a breath but refused to fall. He caught himself on his bad leg, stumbled a second step to shift the weight to his good leg. The distance between the two cats was greater now, the emperor having been pushed back. Zelnir realized the same thing and lowered himself to charge the injured lion, sensing an advantage. As'kai grabbed a knife from his bandolier and threw it. The first missed. As it was supposed to, but the second one Zelnir had not seen or accounted for, sunk deep into his shoulder. A growl followed the blow as he charged. His injury greatly slowed him, and though As'kai was not able to move out of the way, he had enough time to anticipate Zelnir's movements, account for his weight, and take the tiger down with him, claws sinking into his back as they made contact. Blood stained both of their fur along with the sand around them as they traded blows, and wounds. As'kai knew he could not keep this up. His leg was badly wounded and still actively bleeding. If he did not get help soon, he was going to be in grave danger; if he wasn't already. He remembered what he'd said to Ku'tem. "I will not go willingly or easily, I promise you." He would keep this promise to his empress, and would not kid himself he could outsmart a prophecy. If he was to die on those plains, he was going to die an emperor. He was going to make sure the tiger knew it and felt it. As'kai fought harder, biting when he had the access to bite, stabbing when he could get his paws on a knife, and clawing whenever his paws made contact with the soft fur of the tiger's body. He wanted the tiger bloodied for weeks to come. He did not know how long they fought for, but he could feel it when his body started to give. It started with the pounding in his ears as his heart worked harder to circulate his blood. Then a low headache, a fog, a delay in the response of his limbs to his commands. Zelnir seemed to sense it too; the shift in the fight. He started thrashing, whatever Kiel had taught him coming to the forefront as he made strike after strike towards As'kai's stomach. Once As'kai was good and bloodied, and unable to walk, Zelnir reached up and took a sword from where it was strapped on the emperor's back. As'kai tried to get up. He tried to cover the soft underside of his body where any fatal blow might land to kill him, but his body was so shredded his vision already fading as the tiger raised to his knees above him. As'kai swiped at him as he positioned the sword at his heart, and Zelnir merely moved forward, kneeling on the emperor's already battered arm. His other arm had already been injured, most likely dislocated at the shoulder, unusable due to some uncalculated strength within the young tiger. His legs, a strong and second defense, would not respond to his commands — if they even could. Zelnir leveled the sword at the emperor's heart, looking him dead in the eyes. "You won't even let me die standing? Where is your honor?" As'kai's voice shook with the effort of his words.

"Where was your people's honor when they murdered my family for sport?" Zelnir spit. He was bloodied, his fur matted with redness all over. "You do not get to speak of honor to me." Zelnir pressed the tip of the sword into As'kai's chest, making a new cut on a previously unmarked patch of the emperor's battered body. "What say you of your people? And what say you of the balance? Of the debts for my parents' lives?" "Mother Nature will never forgive you for this. Mother Nature knows not of the balances of blood and decay." "Mother Nature knows of the balance of all." The tip of the sword went a little further. "And, Emperor, remember this. You are only one life. And I am not feeling generous. Your guards? They mean nothing. I will be back. I will claim another life, and then the throne. I hear you have sons...and a beautiful empress. Perhaps the next one... will be her." As'kai only had time to shout out half of a broken "NO" before the tiger slid the sword home, straight through the heart of the emperor of the Transvaal Pride. The tiger watched as the life bled out of the emperor's eyes, and then he stumbled back towards the fire where his companions were half cheering, half awed. He collapsed halfway there, succumbing to his wounds.

CHAPTER EIGHT

UNDER NEW RULE

****

Rael and Geo waited anxiously in the training room for word of their father's return. Rael paced the length of the room by the doorway, unable to focus on much of anything, but the scuff of his feet on the dirt and the pounding of his brother's fists as Geo pounded out combinations into one of their training pads in one of the corners. Imena, Ulan's daughter, sat in the opposite corner of Geo, watching him worriedly as he worked. None of them spoke, the tension thickening the air to the point of being nearly unbreathable. Rael's head reeled with the day's events: his father leaving, Geo's giving up of his place on the throne, the looming notion his father may very well not return home this night. He was only brought out of the spiral when the scuff of his feet was joined by a secondary set from outside in the hallway. He paused his route, glancing back at Geo in time to see his brother approach, taking post at Rael's right shoulder. Even Imena stood wondering who approached. Ulan's white fur appeared in the doorway a moment later, and hope dared to swell in his chest, only to be dashed when he saw the unshed tears in Ulan's eyes. Geo growled, loud, and painful, pushing over the rack of training gear which was next to them. Rael looked at the floor, choked to the point of being unable to speak. Ulan didn't say anything, waiting until they had both composed themselves enough to hear what the spiritual leader had to say. When both princes had returned to him, he shared delicately, "Your father is dead." Rael and Geo shared a pained glance, one that held comfort but a year's worth of training and knowledge, as well as anger and rage at the way this has played out. But they were princes. They knew their role in the pride, knew what it meant to them now that the emperor had fallen. "How can you be sure of such things?" Geo asked. "I saw it in a vision not long ago. Guards have already been dispatched to bring his body home. I'm sorry, my cubs." "Father never told us how twins of the past settled ascensions." Rael stated softly. He hoped Geo would not bring up his statement from earlier in the day. "Nor will I," Ulan said. "You will set a new precedent in the way that you handle it. It is your duty to figure it out." "Figure it out!" Geo spat from his brother's side. Rage was there etched into every plain of his face. "How are we to figure it out when the man who was supposed to teach us has died without even giving us the full grace of the history of what we are?" he snarled. "And to leave us in the hands of someone who knew all of what was to come and did nothing!" "Geo!" Rael warned cutting his brother off. "It's okay, Rael. He is right. I did know. But there was nothing I could have done, Geo. I am a messenger and nothing more." "Then why tell us, if there is no way to prevent it? What of prophecies if there is nothing to do but wait for them to pass?" Geo's chest was heaving now under the rate of his breaths. Imena came up to his side placing a paw on his shoulder. Geo glanced at her and closed his eyes. He opened them a moment later and turned back to Ulan, then to his brother. "I said it before, and I'll say it again. I won't have any part in this game, these... these... politics. Rael can be seated at the throne. I want nothing more than to see that tiger fall." "Geo!..." "...I won't hear it brother!" Geo shouted to Rael, placing his paw over Imena's, then moving them both from his shoulder. "I'm to speak with the generals and rally the army. The tiger will be here soon, and we will do nothing but defeat him if I have anything to say about it." With that, he left. Rael watched after his brother, sadness striking him yet again. "Mother says he was grieving even before father died. Now that he is gone, I don't know what he is going to do. He won't stay in a room with any of us long enough to speak of it." "Give him time, Rael. He is young." "We are both young, Ulan." Rael looked at the spiritual leader, his youth and hurt plain and open on his face. "That you are, cub, that you are." Ulan's face reflected the pain back at the young prince. "What are we to do now?" Rael kindly asked, trying his best to maintain the discussion of business. "We must discuss this with your mother." Rael's eyes widened, flickering to Imena and then refocusing on Ulan. "Mother." Without waiting for a reply from the spiritual leader, he fled from the room, following the spiraling hallway up, up, up, until he reached the throne room where he knew his mother had been waiting since his father had left. He found her perched in her throne, her face damp with the tears of her grief. His father's throne sat empty, a hulking reminder of the absence which will never again be filled. "Rael!" The empress named as soon as he entered the room. The prince raced to his mother, hugging her tightly as the two of them took moments to weep. It was a long while before they pulled themselves together long enough to step away. "Where is your brother?" Ku'tem asked, glancing behind her eldest twin. Rael shook his head. "He left after Ulan shared the news. I don't know where he's gone." Ku'tem hung her head. "He is taking all of this very hard." Rael nodded. "He is ceding his spot on the throne." She looked back up at him. "He can't." "He's said it twice now, Mother. I don't know what I am to do other than operate under the impression at this moment that he does not want it." Ku'tem sighed. "What are we to do, Rael?" "We are to prepare for war. Tomorrow, we will announce the death of Emperor As'kai and the ascension of the heirs. We will send messengers out as well so the prides around the plains know, and also know we are preparing for war. Killing an emperor is not an act to be taken lightly, and we are not treating it as anything less than what it is: a full throttled threat to the entire empire. "No one will get into this castle or launch another attack without us knowing about it,

Mother. Geo is in close communication with the generals, and he, myself, the advisors, and the fellow pride leaders will be in close contact, I promise." Rael informed his mother. She beamed at him. "So it is you who will ascend the throne, Rael? Alone?" "I will be seated for the time being. Geo is more prepared for war than I am. He will be strong to lead our warriors."

Rael worried after his brother and hoped he was with the warriors preparing. "When the time comes of peace following the war, we may rediscuss." Rael looked to the door, hoping his brother might walk in and confirm this, but he did not come, and his unasked question was met with no answer. Rael turned back to his mother, relief hitting him again because she was truly in one piece. She was okay, save for the hole where her husband used to stand at her side. "Is war really the answer?" Ku'tem asked. "The pride will be mourning your father immensely. Is war something we can truly handle right now?" "It is something they are going to have to handle." Another voice declared, coming into the room. It was Ulan, having finally caught up to the running prince. Imena was just behind him. "The tiger will come whether we are prepared for him or not. He wishes to gain control of the plains, and he will pursue this goal to one end or another. Killing the emperor was not enough. He wants the control for himself, not just a shift of power. "And the tiger..., he heals as we speak." Ulan continued. "As he heals, there are others around the plains who send word of allies. Before the battle with your father, the tiger went around to as many others as he could and sent them back to Kiel's village. It is working as their hub, and they are rallying. Even those who previously did not wish to fight, who even sided against Zelnir, are now taking team with him. He is persuasive, scarily so, I fear. This war is no longer just between that tiger and we Transvaals. There is no avoiding it. Enemies are coming. As soon as their numbers can unite, they will descend, and we must be prepared." "I want the council convened at once," Rael instructed. "Imena, find my brother please. Tell him to bring the current general. There is a power shift coming, and I need everyone to understand." Imena and Ulan nodded and left to gather the requested members of the pride. Ku'tem came to her son's shoulder, resting a paw on him as she affirmed, "You are going to be a mighty emperor, Rael. Just as your father suspected." "We were supposed to rule together." Rael expressed tenderly, looking out into the hallway as if he could see his brother. "I do not want to take this from him." "He's given it freely." Says their Mother. Rael only shook his head. "It is a role I bear with honor to my father. But it is not a role I will revel in, Mother." "It is your compassion that is going to make you a fine leader, Rael." Rael merely kissed his mother's cheek, and turned to his father's throne. My throne, he thought to himself. Tall and looming, with ornate swirls carved into the wooden backing. It was tall and regal as an emperor's seat should be, and spoke of the years their father had been seated upon it. With a steadying breath, Rael approached the seat, then turned around and stood before it, the flat part of it brushing the back of his knees. Slowly, the generals, advisors, Ulan, and Geo entered the throne room, standing around the dais as they had when As'kai had sat here just several days before.

Rael had snuck into a meeting only once, many years before when he was just a young cub, and seen the way the lions in the room had looked to his father with respect. It was the same manner in which the lions all looked up to him now. I will do what I must to fill the role you left behind, Father, Rael thought. And with a nod to his circle of advisors, Rael sat down upon his throne.

CHAPTER NINE

NEWS SPREADS

****

"Word just came of the emperor's death, Na'uul." Waerik shared as he entered the war room two days later. Na'uul had spent many days there since the initial meeting with his generals and had practically lived in the room since his return from the Transvaal Castle. He plotted the before — what was to happen to get the tiger to side with him, to make them allies, to make him see they were on the same side — and the after, when all was his to rule. "That was quick!" Na'uul expressed as he was unable to keep the surprise off his face, as he assessed his second in command. "Perhaps we should convene the generals. I feel there is much to do now that the emperor has fallen." "Very well, Waerik, summon them. Quickly." Na'uul turned back toward the window as his second returned to the hallway to gather the others. "The emperor, dead?" Na'uul thought. He had been imagining this day for ages, and yet hearing those words — so soon, too, after seeing and interacting with him — was something of a surreal experience. And to have seen the twins and knowing now that one of them was seated in his father's place. Perhaps getting on the throne was going to be easier than he thought.

As the first of his generals filed in, Na'uul took his seat at the head of the table. It wasn't long before the lot of them were once again settled around the oval strategy table. "Waerik, enlighten the generals, please." Na'uul prompted. Waerik nodded, standing. "Messengers came to the compound today to inform us Emperor As'kai of the Transvaals has been killed, and Prince Rael is to ascend the throne in his place. The king was found on the plains not far from the tiger village where their spiritual leader resides in, near the east. It appears that he was in a great battle, where he was stabbed in the heart with his own sword."

BYRON S. DOWLING SR.

"Have we any idea who did this?" Myre asked. "Ulan, the spiritual leader of the lions and one who is in frequent communication with the Transvaals, said it cannot be confirmed, but many suspect it to be the rogue tiger. He killed many of the Transvaal guards, and he has been working his way towards the leader's throne this entire time. It would make sense that it would be him." Na'uul stroked his chin for a long moment. "Do we know where the tiger has fled? Do we know if he has gotten any of our correspondences?" "We've already sent messages to him." Nayme assured, the shock evident in his voice. "Nayme." Na'uul threw him a sharp look. "The emperor's body isn't even cold, and you've already been trying to speak with his killer. It's treason!" His son exclaimed. "We were in correspondence before the emperor was killed, child," Waerik said to him, and then to the Na'uul leader, "Yes, they've reached him. He has sent none back with our messengers, however." "Father —" "Your morality has no place here, Nayme." "Father, this is not about morality. This is about being an enemy to the throne." "We will not be enemies to it once I am in control," Na'uul announced. "You think I cannot keep a tiger barely out of his adolescence under wraps?" "He just murdered the emperor." Nayme pressed. "What do you think he will do to you once you've served your purpose?" "The emperor was weak." Na'uul said darkly, "Weak willed and weak bodied. No tiger will have control over me." Nayme stared at his father for a long time but said nothing more. "The messages, Waerik," Na'uul said, trying to get the meeting back on track. "Yes. Some have made it to him, as the messengers reported delivering them and watching him read, but he's yet to send anything back. We are tracking his whereabouts with spies and the network. However, he's currently back in his village, being tended to by his allies there. Their numbers have grown drastically since he ran from there a little more than a week ago."

Waerik reported. "I want another message sent out tonight asking for council with him. Tell him he's permitted guards if it so suits him. Give him the grace of knowing what the meeting is about. Send only the most trusted guards Waerik, and make sure that spiritual tiger is nowhere to be found when those messengers land. He is in Ulan's ear, who is right in the ear of the Transvaals. We do not want them to hear of anything before we are on their front step in full battle readiness." "Right away, Na'uul." "Generals, is there any input which need be made on what is to unfold here?" Na'uul asked the others in the room. When no one said anything, Na'uul nodded once. "Good. Prepare the armies then. I suspect we are going to be riding into battle very soon. Dismissed." The generals fled as quickly as they had come, all except for Nayme. "Father, if the king is dead, that means the cubs —" "I know what it means, Nayme. It means a lot of things for me as well." Nayme sighed. "Father, are you not concerned about this drive for the throne?" "I deserve the throne," Na'uul practically snarled. "I am tired of living under his thumb." Nayme made his way toward the door. "He is no longer at the helm of the ship. It should not be about what you deserve, but about what the people deserve. Consider this."

*****

Word came from the tiger four days later, agreeing to meet at his village only as he was still too weak to move. He promised Kiel would be away from the temple at the time of his arrival, and no one who saw Jaal would tell the Transvaals they had been anywhere near the tigers. It was Waerik, as it always was, who had brought the message to Na'uul, along with his personal feelings on the matter. "I don't trust him, Na'uul. I don't think it is a good idea to go right into the heart of his territory." "Territory?" "Army base, headquarters, whatever suits you to call it Na'uul, it is not safe for us to go there. We cannot hold our ground if we are right in the center of all they know." "I don't disagree with him." A third voice contributed to the conversation. Ex'ne. He stood in the doorway, poised as if he were prepared to leave and come back later, but the chance of leaving the conversation without his input would have been sin. "Ex'ne," Na'uul addressed. "please speak more on that." "Forgive me for eavesdropping, Na'uul, but there is no benefit to us going to his place of residence. There is only benefit to him. We do not know the tiger's area of the plains well, and we have no allies that far north. Our spies have seen far too little to be able to plot out an effective assault should things go south. There is no way for us to be effectively prepared should he decide we are enemies rather than allies." The general stood sturdily, with his paws clasped behind his back, his head raised confidently as he spoke. He was never one to shy away from giving a battle opinion. It was what made him so good. "It is common knowledge the fight with As'kai put the tiger down, however," Na'uul said. "It may be fair to assume that he cannot travel this far. So if he cannot come here, we cannot go there, what would you suggest we do to progress these alliance negotiations?" "A neutral middle ground." Ex'ne replied quickly. "Neutral will always be the best option in these scenarios. Neutral means not here and not there. We can pick a place we know well, station spies, and hidden guard in the event that he strikes." "So you mean to lie to the cat we wish to side with?" Ex'ne lowered his gaze, only enough to meet eyes with his leader. "Is that not what war is, all just one big game? If he does not go into this expecting to get played..., if you do not go into this with the expectation of getting played..., then you should not be going to war." Na'uul sized up his general for a long moment, turned to Waerik, then nodded. "Waerik, send message to the tiger that it is not in our best interest to go to the heart of his . . . pride? Clan? Whatever you decide a group of tigers should be called, I'm not sure. I've never been part of one." The lion chuckled to himself at his small joke. "Tell him a neutral location halfway between each of our lands will be preferable for us. There is unclaimed land a day's walk from us that we've mapped extensively for a rainy day. Suggest this spot as neutrally as you can and see if he bites." Waerik nodded, and made to leave, edging around the battle-hardened Ex'ne as he did so. Ex'ne watched the second in command leave, but did not follow. "Is there something else you need?" Na'uul asked. "Yes, Na'uul. I apologize. I've had some of my lower ranks gathering all the information they could about numbers and running messages to the lions at the Transvaal Castle. It appears as though one of the twins — Geo, the dark-maned one — is now commanding their armies. He has them training rigorously each day: our men, Anpher's men, and their own. They run combat, strategy, and defense. I fear… I fear there may have been a bit of underestimation on our part, about how well the Transvaals can fight." Na'uul had turned his attention away from the general to look out the window, as if he could see straight across the plains into his enemy's territory. "What is it that you are suggesting?" "What if we are underprepared, as we had once suspected?" Ex'ne posed. Na'uul snarled, turning on his general. "We are recruiting the tiger who killed the mighty Transvaal emperor. The general who commands that army is nothing more than a child, and the men who make it up are playing. They have never set foot on the battlefield. They see themselves as heroes because they wear the clothes of warriors, but they are in costume. They know nothing of what it is like to fight." "Forgive me, Na'uul, but our warriors do not know either. The last war that happened took place nearly fifty years ago, long before many of us were even born. That war happened between the Pynme, which devastated them even more than the Pride Wars of a century ago, and the Fenwyre. It is what made the Fenwyre so powerful, for the Pynme prisoners had a choice of joining their ranks or being executed. Since then, any Pynme born to the Fenwyre Pride have had the choice of fighting or fleeing. Many have chosen to stay, as they know nothing else. If anything, they are the only ones who know of struggle and war. Anpher's men are the only ones prepared for this war. It is they who give the Transvaals a chance. And remember, they do not fight on our side. They fight on his. With the Transvaal's numbers, and the Fenwyre's skill..., do we stand a chance?" "Leave Ex'ne, and do not come back until you find your faith in your own men." "I am a strategist, Na'uul. I think in strategy." "Then think of a strategy that allows us to win," Na'uul growled. He stared down his general, until there was nothing for the lesser ranked lion to do but bow and exit the room in silence.

*****

Na'uul, Nayme, the generals, and Waerik were suited and waiting at the Jaal Castle door for the guard they were bringing to signal their departure three days later. The tiger had agreed to their neutral location, and they were to meet the following day at dusk to discuss their allyship. "Do we have everything?" Waerik asked the Jaal leader one final time. "We have the generals, weapons, and food. That should be enough for this trip, Waerik. Stop working yourself up." "These are anxious times, Na'uul. Forgive me." The Jaal leader only nodded in response. A moment later, the horn signaled the leader's departure. Nara, Na'uul's daughter, stood to the side with some of the other pride members, waving her father and brother off. Nayme gave her a soft smile, a smile that faded until his face was cold as stone when he turned back to forward facing. Na'uul knew this was not a trip Nayme wanted to take and not a trip he was willing to take. He had only come because he held on to some false notion that he could convince Na'uul to turn away from the tiger as an ally.

The journey to the neutral lands took a day so long as they kept moving. The intention was to arrive at dawn of the next day so they could situate defenses before the tiger and his troop arrived. Ex'ne was insistent on precautions, his distrust of the tiger more pronounced with every mention of the young cat. The Jaal made good time, stopping only to hydrate and eat when necessary, to rest for several hours during the hottest points of the day, with the hope of saving energy so they could travel through some of the coolest parts of the night. By the time the sun started to light the sky on the horizon, though the sun itself was not yet visible, the troop could see the neutral land in the distance. "We're getting close." Na'uul announced to the lot of them. "Another hour's walk and we should be there." They made it just as the sun was cresting over the farthest hills. Ex'ne immediately broke off from the group, running the perimeter of the land to determine where the best places would be for them to hide away some of the guards without being seen. "The tigers are expected to come from here," He pointed to clarify, "so we should hide guards there, there, and there," He indicated the spots, "to keep them hidden as the tigers approach. They will also have vantage points of the deliberations if they hide in those spots, so it will benefit us best." "And it will benefit us best to hide them now. It looks like the tigers might have had the same idea as us." Waerik nodded his head in the direction Ex'ne indicated their potential allies would come from. A cloud of dust, unavoidable in the arid conditions of some parts of the savannah, indicated someone was approaching. From the size of the dust plume, it was reasonable to assume there were many. Ex'ne immediately fell into his role, ordering those who had come as backup into their hideaways.

The other generals circled around Na'uul as representatives of the royal standing, and also as a first line of defense for their leader. Nayme was hidden slightly behind them, still visible but protected. Waerik had warned against bringing his only heir to this should it become a bloodbath, but Na'uul insisted this was how Nayme was to learn how to rule when his time came for the throne. The rest of the guard fanned out behind them, making a half circle in the attempt to make it seem like they were the only other defense they had brought. The more the tiger felt trusted from the beginning, Na'uul believed, the better this would go.

The Jaal only waited a few minutes before the first of the tigers hit the neutral land. Similar to the formation the lions had, the tigers who approached fanned out in a half-circle along the far side of the territory. Five lined either side of the make-shift entrance, before three came directly forward, sizing Na'uul and his generals up before splitting so their leader could make his entrance. The tiger still wore bandages from his fight with the emperor, almost a week prior now, but he was walking upright. Na'uul had expected him to still be in need of some aid, but was pleased to see this was not the case. He had a gash on his face which was healing pink, a key indication it would scar, and one of his paws was still patchy where fur had been taken off — perhaps bitten off, from the way the pattern of markings looked. Even Na'uul had to suppress a shudder at that. The emperor had fought dirty, it seemed.

Finally, all movement in the area ceased, and the tigers and the lions sized each other up — big cat against big cat, waiting to see who would make the first move. Na'uul could feel the tension rolling off of his generals, all poised to pounce at the first sign of any danger. The tiger's guard appeared the same, with half of them sneering just at the proximity of his lions. He almost liked it, the tension. Perhaps it would help to keep all of them at bay when he ruled. Na'uul was the first to break the tension, figuring it was on him since he had been the one to summon everyone. He started with a breeze of a smile. "Thank you for coming all of this way to hear me out," He expressed. "I was intrigued. A lion willing to turn on his own. I had to see it for myself, if nothing else." The tiger declared, crossing his arms over my chest. Na'uul's smile grew a little darker. "I feel there is much you do not know about us lions." A low growl escaped from one of the tiger's closer guards, but he held up his hand and the sound cut off. "If you are here to court me into being an ally, it might serve you best not to condescend me," The tiger spoken lowly. "I apologize. It is just that I have not met someone so young, yet so ambitious, in a long time, not since, perhaps, myself." The tiger smiled at his words, and a chuckle rumbled through the guard of tigers which stood behind him. "My name is Na'uul, leader of the Jaal Pride on the far side of the plains."

Na'uul held out his hand. "Zelnir. I live in the eastern tiger village." "Brought in by a spiritual leader, only to betray him. Word does get around." Na'uul revealed, eyeing the tiger again as they shook hands. "We were supposed to meet at dusk tonight," The tiger, Zelnir, detailed, retracting his paw. "so imagine my surprise when we arrived early, and you were already here." "I don't have to imagine it. I experienced it myself. But I suppose, let me make this my first point as to why we might be good allies. We can both agree to the benefit of the element of surprise." Zelnir's smile widened, and perhaps it might have been imagined, but Na'uul thought he saw a spark of amusement in the young tiger's eyes. "Tell me, Na'uul, why you want to ally with us tigers so badly. And more importantly, why should I trust you will not betray us for your own gains and advantages." "It's simple. We want the same things. The Transvaals dethroned and out of power." Zelnir chuckled, low and humorless. "A slight misunderstanding, I think. I do not want just the Transvaals out of power. I want all lions out of power. Do you see the difference?" Na'uul nodded. "I can work with that as well. I know you do not have the numbers to take them on." "I just killed their emperor. If they fight anything like him, I feel I do not need numbers." "You will." It was Ex'ne, stepping forward from the line of Na'uul's generals. "I am Na'uul's best strategist, and I have warriors and spies on the inside. It has been brought to my attention that you will need the numbers. They are being trained as we speak, are better fighters than we anticipated, and they have the best warriors in the kingdom on their side." Zelnir sized Ex'ne up, then turned back to Na'uul. "And you intend to fight on our side, then cede the throne to me? And that's it?" "Well..." Zelnir guffawed. "Now we are getting somewhere. Please, sit. I think that this is going to be fun."

CHAPTER TEN

THE ENEMY APPROACHES

****

Ulan's footsteps echoed in the great hallway as he approached the throne room. Voices floated out toward him through the doorway as he made his way closer. Some he recognized, such as the twins, the empress, and his daughter, though the last surprised him. The rest were a muddling of male voices, most likely the council, guards, and generals, preparing for the war, or even waiting to hear what he had to say when he arrived. Rael had greatly expanded the circle of those who needed to hear news of the impending war since his father's passing. Though he knew many of the guardsmen from the other prides were not privy to how dire the situation truly was, Ulan had cautioned the new emperor about being so openly trusting of their new residents. He had bad feelings about the war which was to come. Anyone who was not

Transvaal was not to be trusted if he had anything to say about it, but he knew that he did not. Though he was a trusted advisor to the throne, the cubs were trying to follow their father's example — and he had trusted Anpher and Na'uul enough to invite their armies into his home. That was enough for his sons to trust them as well. With a steadying breath, Ulan entered the throne room, scanning the faces of the fellow lions that were there. There were about ten of them, milling about and talking among themselves. Ulan nodded to a few of them, smiling when he recognized some of the Transvaal council. When Imena saw him, her face broke out into a smile, and she came off the dais from where she had been standing next to Geo to give him a hug. Geo, Ulan noticed, watched her go, and then turned to his brother to inform him of the spiritual leader's arrival. The emperor turned to Ulan and nodded to him. As if he had spoken, that gesture was enough for the other lions in the room to disperse from their conversations and make their way to the seats surrounding the room. Geo and Rael sat on the dais, where a third throne had been brought in. Rael sat in his father's old throne, with Geo to his right in the newest, and his mother Ku'tem in the throne to his left. She would remain the regent empress until Rael came of age at sixteen and found a bride of his own. Ulan made his way to the last two available seats on the main floor with Imena, when Rael called to him. "Ulan, I would like it if you would sit up here with us this evening. I understand you have news, and it would be helpful if everyone could hear and see you as you deliver it." "Yes sire," Ulan answered, shooting a knowing look at the young emperor. He only turned away, and Ulan felt sorry for him. He was young, too young still to be on the throne, and yet here he was — a duty which was meant to be split between him and his brother, but he was doing it alone. Imena followed him to the dais and took position next to Geo's chair. Ulan noticed how the younger twin was turned slightly away from his brother, from the responsibility which their father had thrown at them. And for a moment — only a moment — Ulan was angry at his long-time friend As'kai for running off to that tiger, for leaving him in charge of the twins like this. They had not even had time to grieve the loss of their father and yet they already sat at the head of their pride.

When Ulan was positioned next to the empress' shoulder, Rael stood and cleared his throat, calling everyone's attention to him, despite the fact that everyone was already watching. "Thank you all for being here. I know this meeting was called at the last minute, but there has been word that our enemy approaches. Ulan?" Rael turned to the spiritual leader, nodding his head then returning to his seat on the throne. Ulan thanked the emperor silently and then stepped forward to address the room. "Kiel showed up at the Western Temple several nights ago while I was there for a routine check-in. He told me the tiger, who is responsible for all of this, Zelnir, had gone into the savannah to meet with a potential ally who was to bring him many recruits. That night, I had a repeat of a dream I had several months ago, only this time, it was clearer, more detailed. They definitely have lions on their side, and there will be many of them. And they are coming soon, within a few days' time. We must prepare quickly." "Do we know how many days exactly?" A voice called into the room. "Or who's the lion they met with!?" Yelled another. Ulan shook his head slowly. "I don't have answers for you, and for that, I am sorry." "Well, how are we..." "...I understand that you are all scared," The emperor vented, standing up beside the spiritual leader, "but Ulan has told us all that he can. What we do know is that the lions here have your backs. Trust only the faces you recognize from this castle on the battlefield. As for when they are coming..., we knew this was a war, and it was to happen soon. There is nothing that we are to do now, but wait for them to arrive, and continue to do what we have been doing, which is train." "And we are well-trained." Geo stated, stepping up beside his brother. "I was trained by my father, the former emperor, who was trained by his father before him. We have won many battles this way, and with our numbers, we will be strong. We can win this." "The emperor was killed with this training," A third voice declared faintly, close to the dais. A darkness fell over the royal family. It was Rael who answered the jab. "We know not how our father died. If you do not trust the ways in which we have prepared, you may leave. But trust that we will no longer recognize you in the eyes of this castle should you return seeking refuge." No one moved a muscle, not even the speaker invited to leave the room. When it was clear no one was going to leave, Rael nodded, and the two brothers returned to their seats. "Ulan, was there anything else?" Geo gently asked. "No, sire." "I am not sire." He replied in the same tone. "You will only address my brother as such." Ulan only nodded in response. "If there is nothing else, then all are dismissed. Geo, take the generals down to the strategist's room and begin to prepare for battle. Tell the trainers to continue leading all of the men in simulation and sparring. I want them rested, but trained as best as they can be by the time the tiger arrives. There are no excuses for our men to be falling behind in any way. Mother, I want you to take the women on one last hunt. Take a section of the guard with you in case the tiger tries to make any moves while you are out. We do not know how long this battle will take, and we will need food for the aftermath as well." The empress nodded. Ulan couldn't help but observe Rael in this moment. He had taken his father's mantel in stride, and he was commanding this room as if he had done so for years. Many had assumed after the fall of the emperor, Ulan would stand as temporary hand to the throne while the empress ran the pride, but it appeared as of yet, to be unnecessary. "Ulan," Rael continued, pulling the spiritual lion's attention back to the present. Rael's gaze softened ever so slightly. "thank you..., for all you have done for us." He gave the spiritual lion a weighty nod, then turned back to his council. "Go. Prepare for war." All of the men in the room rose and bowed as they exited, giving the same amount of respect to Rael as they would As'kai. The room slowly emptied, until only Rael, Geo, Ulan, and Imena remained. "You twins are fine leaders," Ulan admitted to them as he made a slow progression to the door with his daughter. "I wish we weren't," Rael delicately uttered. "Our father should be here." Geo remained silent. Imena laid a comforting paw on Geo's shoulder, a gesture which did not go unnoticed by her father. "I understand your pain." "You will never understand our pain!" Geo hissed. "I have to go prepare. If we do not know when he is coming, then we must act like he is coming now." Geo touched Imena's paw gently, then rose from his throne and exited the room. "He gets better each day," Imena said tenderly, "but it is a slow thing to heal from grief." She approached her father, linking her arm through his. "Come along, Father. We have preparations of our own." Ulan gave one final look of sympathy to the emperor and then followed the tugging of his daughter out into the hallway.

CHAPTER ELEVEN

THE GREAT WAR

****

The tigers and their companion lions came into view around dawn two days after the meeting with Ulan in the throne room. Geo was the first to see them, sitting guard out on the ridge where his father used to take him and his brother to play. They were still a few miles away, just cresting the ridge, but Geo wasted no time racing back to the castle. Those many years of challenging his brother to races finally coming to mean something as his paws pounded the savannah dirt. He made it back to the castle doors in record time. "They're here!" He exclaimed to the closest guard, and that was all it took. The ball of tension the entire castle had been living in for the year since this threat had started to loom exploded. People ran frantically, gathering the children to sequester them away to wherever they felt was safest. The guards ran to gather all those who would be fighting. The empress took her seat on the throne, to watch over the battle and to go down with the castle should it come to that. Geo knew they were prepared. They had been preparing for many months for this, and still, he felt there had not been enough time, and he also felt they were going to get obliterated. Thoughts spiraled through his head as he made his way to the strategy room to find his brother — the emperor. If they lost this battle, their legacy left to them by their father would be for nothing. Centuries of what the lions had built up would be taken to rubble. The tigers would undo everything they had built in an instant, and he knew they would leave no lion loyal to them alive. It would be a genocide.

"Rael." Geo called as he pushed the curtain aside to enter the room. His brother and Geo's two leading generals were at the table discussing last-minute plans. "They're here." Rael assessed his brother, saw through the stoic outside to the panic within, acknowledged it with a look of sympathy, and then nodded in a way only an emperor would. "Okay generals, it seems that it might be time. Get to your men, get to your positions. Geo, get everyone out to meet them as far away from this castle as you can. I don't want to fight in our backyard. The lionesses and cubs do not need to see this." Geo bowed to his brother and then led the two generals out of the room, back down to the main foyer to where the armies now gathered. All stood at attention when he approached, and he barely had a second to feel the disgust he normally did when they looked at him like that. He instructed each man to their sector, dividing them into their appropriate groups, telling them where exactly they were supposed to march, what to expect. Then, when Rael came down from the strategy room and stood before the armies alongside him, a united front as they were always supposed to be, they turned and marched.

*****

Across the plains, the tigers saw as the Transvaal armies left the castle. Na'uul and his lions hid behind the tigers' barricade, hoping to keep their identity hidden for as long as possible. Waerik stood to his left, his son to his right, and the armies they had not spared to the Transvaals stood behind them. According to Ex'ne, all of the lions that had gone to the Transvaals had been informed of when they were to reveal their true alliances, and as of that moment, there was no indication that any of them had revealed themselves as traitors to the Transvaals. Na'uul couldn't help but smile to himself. This whole plan could not have gone any better. The lions on the other side of the plain crept closer, and the tigers in front of Na'uul's men slowed. "We will let them meet us out here," Zelnir yelled as loudly as he could. "We know this area where there are hills and hideaways. If they fall into a divot, we may yet be able to get out, to the side, or even behind them." There was a muttering of agreement through the crowd. No one dared challenge Zelnir here. Even Ex'ne seemed to agree with his strategy. Everyone was onboard except for Nayme. "Father," Na'uul's son said softly, quietly enough that the tigers a few rows ahead would not hear. "this is the last chance to reconsider this. Before the Transvaals label us traitors. I beg you do not go forward with this." "Those twins are no better fit to rule than their father, Nayme — less so even. These tigers will help us to get them off the throne and get us into power." "These tigers want the power for themselves. We will get nothing for this, but exiled by the other prides. When the tigers turn on us, we will have no aid. We will be obliterated — same as all the rest." "You are too pessimistic, Nayme. This is the type of situation where breed doesn't matter. Cats help cats." Nayme's eyes watched his father for a long time, studying him. "Cats will never help cats without a price,

Father. This is one thing I have learned from history. Betraying one's own will always come at a cost." "The Transvaals are not our own. The Jaals are. And I will do whatever I can to make this better for them." "Do not kid yourself into thinking you are doing this for them. You want power —" "Lower your voice," Na'uul snarled. "you will get us killed before there is even a war." "It is not my actions which risk our lives, and I beg you to consider." Then Nayme turned away. Na'uul snarled at him again, then fought his way forward, towards where Zelnir stood at the front of the pack. "How much longer do you think?" "Not long now," Zelnir answered. "we need them to be slightly closer, until we have the upper hand, and then we will descend." Na'uul nodded. "Who will make the first move?" "I'm sure it will be us. They will try to negotiate and wager with us, talk us out of a war, but I will have none of it. We will run them as soon as the discussion ceases." Na'uul nodded, and they lapsed into silence.

It was not long after when they realized Zelnir had been wrong. As soon as they crested the closest ridge, where it would be a seen attack, but one which would not get them slaughtered immediately, the Transvaal lions charged. There was no discussion. Right at the front of the charge stood the emperor and his brother, rage clear on their faces as they ran directly towards Zelnir. Na'uul saw the moment when Rael recognized him, his eyes falling away from the tiger's leader to the lion's face. Even as he ran, his brow furrowed in confusion, and then tightened as his anger grew. Na'uul's smile grew wicked. He flicked an eyebrow back at Rael, then raised his head to the sky and bellowed with all of his strength, "ATTACK!" Then he watched as all of the lions he had sent to the Transvaals turned towards the lions running besides them and began cutting them down. Geo had just reached the rise where he and Zelnir stood when the clanging of metal behind them caused the royal twins to turn, leaving them open to attacks from the tigers in front who now charged them. "Geo, it's a play! Na'uul!" He heard Rael shout to his brother. The young general roared and returned to his charge, fighting his way towards Na'uul instead of Zelnir. Na'uul welcomed the challenge. It had been a long time since he had a worthy opponent. All around him, he heard big cats snarling and clawing at one another, listened as powerful jaws clenched and tore at flesh and bone and swords clashed and clanged, meeting fiercely and unforgiving. But his eyes stayed locked on the charging general, cutting down the tigers and Jaal warriors that kept him from Na'uul. It was a glorious thing to behold, the rage. Na'uul would enjoy every second of cutting him to pieces. And then he heard a roar of pain, of panic, beside him. "Father!" Na'uul broke eye contact with the Transvaal general, turning to his left, to where his son's voice called to him. He saw one of Zelnir's tigers charge and pinned his son to the ground, snapping at his neck.

Na'uul started to move toward him, drawing his sword and working his way through the battle towards where his son struggled to fight off his opponent. Then a second sword came up, then straight down through the orange and black cat. Na'uul's gaze rose to where Waerik stood over his son. He helped roll the dead cat off his son, then helped Nayme to stand. Both men looked at Na'uul, Waerik with a nod, Nayme with a look of warning. Na'uul couldn't deny the slight weariness that settled in his gut the moment that he saw the tiger hovering over his son, but he had little time to analyze it, because the next moment, he felt four paws and claws in his back, and then he was face down in the dirt, a growl reverberating in his head as they both went over. As soon as he was planted on the ground, the weight left his body, allowing him to roll to his feet. Geo, the Transvaal general, crouched two feet in front of him, sword now drawn in one hand, the other poised on the ground. His teeth were bared, eyes narrowed as he took in the older lion. He was still small, childlike in body, but his face was cruel in a way that only age and experience could allow. "I should've known." The general declared with a low growl behind each of his words. "You always had a plot, a plan, something to say. You were always searching for a way to undermine my father. Now you seek to undermine my brother, and you do it by siding with them. I should've known." "But you didn't, cub." Na'uul spat. "And now we are here. Your men will be slaughtered, and I will be on the throne." "He will be on the throne. Tigers work for themselves. They will use you to decimate us, and then take what they wish." Na'uul scoffed. "You sound like my son." "Your son is a wise man. I have heard him speak before." "You youth have no idea what you speak of." "We know more than you think," Geo stated, and then he charged. His sword came up while his clawed paw went low, going for the throat and the soft underside of Na'uul's body all at once.

Na'uul blocked both and stepped away, but Geo was already there, using the momentum of his first attack to keep him moving forward, swinging and slashing with each step. All around them, the sounds of battle continued to rage, but Geo did not flinch once, as if he was meant for this. He met each of Na'uul's strikes, already countering it with his own before Na'uul had completely finished his follow through. Dozens of movements were shared between them, with less than half meeting their mark. Both cats were breathing heavily and still neither yielded. Geo managed to land a blow to Na'uul's shoulder with his sword, and the older lion hissed. The sound only seemed to reinvigorate the younger lion, and the fight ramped up in intensity once again. Na'uul's energy was starting to wan, and he feared for the first time perhaps Nayme had been right, that he had underestimated the Transvaals. But then Rael called Geo's name. "Geo, they're slaughtering us!" Na'uul took the opportunity of the younger cat's distraction to kick him in the back, sending him sprawling forward. Geo recovered quickly, but it was clear the blow had hurt. He worked his way back to his feet, already back to mid-swing when his brother called for him again. This time he did not turn away, but Na'uul heard as his own name was called. It was Waerik. "Na'uul, they're turning on us!" Geo and Na'uul met eyes over their crossed swords, and a look of understanding which he never thought he would have with a Transvaal lion seemed to pass between them. Without moving their blades, both lions turned to their name call. Na'uul saw Waerik parry a blow from one of the tigers, and then expanded his view from his second to see that all across the battlefield, both to his lions and to the Transvaal's side of the battlefield, the tigers were fighting indiscriminately. They had turned, just at Nayme said they would. Na'uul turned his head towards where he last saw Zelnir and saw him caught in battle with Rael. Both were bloodied, but Zelnir had a sickening smile on his face, as if he knew something that the whole of the battlefield still did not. As if sensing his gaze, Zelnir's head turned, and his eyes locked on Na'uul's. The all-knowing smile turned to one of pure malice. "Your son is smart." Zelnir called over the tin of war, "Listen next time." Na'uul's eyes widened. Suddenly, he did not hear the sound of fighting, of battle, but the sound of slaughter. His men had been instructed to fight the Transvaals only. He was helping the tigers in committing their own genocide. "No." Na'uul whispered, "This wasn't how this was supposed to go." Geo seemed to sense his turmoil and lowered his sword just a millimeter. "Na'uul, there is time to make this right." Na'uul raised his head to the royal general. "How?" "Help my brother and I defeat him. We will give you amnesty if you help us win this." "How will I know that you, too, will not turn on me?" Geo snarled. "We rule in the ways of our father. Those that do what is right for the entire empire are no enemy to us, so long as they continue to prove it. Help us stop this slaughter and we will grant you pardon. But only if you help to stop this now." Na'uul looked at the young cub in front of him, listening to the clanging of metal around him continue. Then he looked back to his son, where he continued to fight alongside Waerik, surrounded not by Transvaals, but by tigers who were supposed to be their allies. Na'uul turned back to the general and nodded, then as loudly as he could, he yelled, "JAAL! THE TIGERS ARE THE ENEMY! SPREAD THE WORD!" Those closest to him looked up, then started charging the tigers on the battlefield, screaming, "TIGERS ARE THE ENEMY!" As they ran. In an instant, the tides of the battle were turning. Zelnir looked up, watched as the tigers were swarmed by the remaining lions, then seemed to laugh. About what, Na'uul didn't know, but he no longer wished to speculate. "On three, we charge him." Geo instructed as quietly as he could without being drowned out by the battle around them. Na'uul nodded. Geo counted down. When the cub said three, both lions turned and ran as fast as they could towards the leader of the tigers. Rael turned, eyes wide, but seemed to see something in his brother's face because he turned back to his opponent, matching his brother's strike blow for blow as the two charging lions reached the already dueling opponents. Zelnir was still laughing, only this time Na'uul could hear him as he spoke. "It's already too late for you. Three against one — army and foes — and still you will lose." The three lions only fought harder. Even as Zelnir held his smile and his stance, Na'uul could see as his strength started to wan, could see as he got more overwhelmed when the strikes of each of the lions grew less synchronized, more sporadic. The twins seemed to realize the pattern, too, as they started to time their strikes to purposefully not match up with his or with each other's. Zelnir's gaze flicked from each of theirs, until Na'uul had an idea, and slowly started backing off on his strikes. Older and admittedly less skilled then the other two — who were younger and a better match for the tiger — Na'uul let the twins pick up the slack of his strikes. Geo shot him a warning glance, but Na'uul shook his head. I'm not leaving the fight. Keep him distracted, he tried to convey. It seemed to work. Geo's next strike was even more advanced than the others he had been using — even in his fight against Na'uul. When Zelnir was thoroughly distracted by the twins' blows, Na'uul was able to slip around behind the tiger, and with a mighty swing of his sword, he cut down on the back of both of the tiger's knees, sending him pitching forward with a painful roar. Immediately, the two brothers put their swords to either side of his neck, pinning him to the ground, while Na'uul leaned forward and picked up Zelnir's sword from him, out of his reach. "How dare you? Hitting a lion from behind. Cowards, all of you." "Surrender, Zelnir, and we won't slaughter you right here," Rael calmly announced. "Surrender? I am winning this war. I will never surrender to the likes of you," He snarled. "You aren't winning anymore," Na'uul said. He looked across the battlefield to see that, finally, there were more lions than tigers standing. Most tigers were matched two to one with lions, and they were falling fast. Some tigers were on their knees in their own surrender. "No," Zelnir growled. "this wasn't supposed to happen. I had it all planned." "Surrender," Rael repeated. "And be slave to you? I would rather die," Zelnir spat. The twins looked at each other as if coming to an understanding, and then stepped forward as if ready to sheer their swords together. But Na'uul held up his hand. In their meetings in the days prior, Zelnir had revealed to him some personal information which might be useful now. "I require heirs, for when my time passes. And so, while in Kiel's village, I took a wife. I should expect that once I take the throne, she will be respected as any empress would," Zelnir had said during their negotiations. "What about your wife?" Na'uul now asked. "Will she not mourn you?" "I care not for what she needs. I took her for what she can give to me." Zelnir proclaimed, but Na'uul knew it wasn't true. He had seen something in his face when he'd spoken of her, the same thing he was sure others saw on his face when he spoke of his own wife, several years dead now. "Zelnir, if you do not surrender, they will kill you." Na'uul repeated. "No," Rael stated. "we've got him captured. That's enough. If we kill him, we are no better than him. We will take him captive regardless. But you, Na'uul, will take him to your castle to guard. He murdered our father. I want him nowhere near our people." "Brother, is that wise? Na'uul and he were allies." "He turned on us, slaughtered my people as well as yours. He is no ally of mine." Na'uul reassured the twins. "We need to end the fighting." Rael spoke to his brother. "And find a way to restrain him." Added Geo. Rael looked to his brother for a long time before he nodded. "He will go to the dungeons under the castle under consistent guard." Na'uul nodded and looked up and caught eyes with Waerik, who was no longer fighting, but scoping the battlefield. Na'uul waved his second in command to his location. When he arrived, he instructed, "Stay here with the emperor and help restrain the tiger. The general and I are to find restraints and end the war." "There is not much war left to end, luckily." Waerik gestured out towards where the battle once raged. There was a smattering of couples still fighting across the battlefield, but many of the lions were already tending to the fallen, while others were still gathering the remaining tigers into a herd to be dealt with as one. Na'uul thanked his second, and then with the general, they headed off around the battlefield to take care of what little there was left to be done.

EPILOGUE

THE RETURN OF THE PEACE

****

It took several days after the war to make note of all of the dead and cage all of the tigers. Zelnir went into the dungeons at the Transvaal Castle under strict guard, while the other tigers were dispersed among the Transvaal and Fenwyre dungeons to be watched and guarded. The Jaal were still not to be trusted, and guards from the Transvaal pride were also sent to watch them under strict patrols. Word was sent to Anpher of all the lions lost, and of the communal burial of all of the dead to happen in a week's time, inviting all of the family members and royals to attend to honor those lost in the unnecessary war. There were those who were unhappy with the mercy shown to the tigers. Many wished to see him executed for the lives lost, and for the murder of the beloved As'kai, but there were many others still who saw the act of mercy as an honorarium to their fallen emperor.

In the days which followed the war, Rael and Geo were informed of their coronation and swearing in for emperor and general — respectively — would be held at the Great Festival of the Plains, a bi-annual celebration that would occur in the coming months. It would be a time to honor their father and give them time to settle on the throne, and in their new roles, as well as gain information and guidance from Ulan as they were thrust into the position with preparation abruptly. It would also give them time to pause. to grieve, and be young for a moment before the total responsibility of the empire was thrust upon them. Their mother and Ulan would work closely with them to help them return the peace after the war.

Most of this information was translated to the empire via letters and messengers who were sent from the castle to the other prides, and much of it was met with praise. But most of the news was met with disdain at the Jaal Pride. "I can't believe those twins are still somehow going to take the throne. They almost lost that war." Na'uul said to Waerik one night when it was just the two of them in the strategy room. "Na'uul, they are the rightful heirs, and they granted us a pass after we openly betrayed them and sided with a traitor to the throne." "Yes, a huge mistake," Na'uul agreed nodding, "I admit the tiger was not my best move, but it doesn't mean I now simply agree with the Transvaals being the leaders, or agree they handled all of this well. Without my armies, and without me, they would never have won. It is I who took the tiger to his knees, I who ended the fighting when I turned my men back against the tigers..." "...Na'uul, their father was killed by that tiger," Waerik warned, "have compassion. They are young." "That is my point, Waerik. They are young. Too young to be on the throne. Not just by my standing, but by law. Their mother acts as regent, and all are being counseled by Ulan, who is just As'kai, but with a spiritual undertone," Na'uul scowled, "and so while everyone is returning to the Transvaal complacency, while that spiritual leader, and a female, now run the prides, I will be plotting the overthrow for real. I have had inside men. I know how the castle works..." "...Na'uul, you have just come off of defeat. They have guards here, watching you. We are all hurting. We lost many men in battle. Please, reconsider." "There is nothing to reconsider. That throne is to be sat upon by the strongest leader. Again and again, I prove myself to be the strongest, and to do what is necessary for my people to set us up for the most success. So, come the festival, and what follows, I will make a second attempt at the throne, and I will win it." "And what if your men will not stand behind you this time?" "They will." Na'uul stated, "We all try to deny it, but we all crave power. If I promise them power, they will be unable to turn away." Waerik shook his head at his leader, standing up from the table. "You are tying us into knots, Na'uul." "I am getting us what we all rightly deserve." Na'uul rose from the table as well. He was making his way across the room to the table, where he looked out over his people, seeing the same dirt towns and dirt roads as he had before — as he did every time he looked out from this room. "We all stand on our own as prides, Na'uul. They are rulers only to keep peace among us." "Well, I do not have peace, I have anger. I win them a war and still my people have nothing. We are being overseen by children. My son undermines my abilities. I will show them. I will get them what they deserve, and it all starts with me getting that throne."

UNFAZED PUBLISHING
YOUR MIND IS OUR BUSINESS

WWW.UNFAZEDPUBLISHING.COM

WHAT'S YOUR STORY ?